PROLOGUE BY PEPY I, PHARAOH OF EGYPT

Heiroglyphics on papyrus, a letter from Pepy I, Pharaoh of Egypt, dying, to his son, soon to be Pepy II, who will inherit a kingdom at the age of six:

Remember, my son, that Egypt is like a poppy abloom in a red desert. The lush Delta marshes are its petals; its curving stem is the Nile.

Nurture the blossom.

Beware of the roots: the Black Dwarves, agile dancers but silent killers; the Minikins of Yam, who hurl their ivory boomerangs with the skill of Egyptian bowmen; the souls of the dead which abide in the gems of the living, amethyst, sard, and sardonyx.

Shun the unholy South: murderous Set and his crew of demons (murderers of my father), whom I, Pepy I, have exorcised from the North with incantation and prayer; the insatiable sphinx with the wings of a bird and the haunches of a lion; the four-legged sta with the head of an asp; the monster goddess Taueret, who raises her sword to eclipse the sun; the amorous succubi who come to men in the night and leave them forever dissatisfied with mortal women; and, insubstantial as mist, insidious as smoke,

the Green Melancholy.

Thomas Burnett Swann

THE MINIKINS OF YAM

Illustrated by GEORGE BARR

DAW BOOKS, INC.
DONALD A. WOLLHEIM, PUBLISHER

1301 Avenue of the Americas
New York, N. Y.   10019

FIRST PRINTING, FEBRUARY 1976

1 2 3 4 5 6 7 8 9

PRINTED IN U.S.A.

PART

I

Chapter I

Egypt.

Chemmis.

The summer palace of Pharaoh.

A gatekeeper who was a friend; a gate which opened as silently as the jaws of a hippopotamus. . . .

Pepy II, Pharaoh of Egypt, lord of the Twin lands, earthly incarnation of the sun god Ra, preferred the moon to the sun, luna moths to dragonflies. Once the brazen chariot of Ra had sunk into the west, he was no longer a child of twelve who must act like a man but whose only power was his inherited name. He was Harpocrates, the Child of Silence, who visited his people to feed the poor and companion the lost and forlorn; to do what a boy on a throne could only entrust to his sister, Henna, and Ayub, the priest of Ra.

First he must hide his kingly trappings and become a shadow, an eddy of wind, an invisibility. Red-haired and ruddy, he carried the blood of the northern barbarians in his veins and he must smudge his face and darken his hair with umber from the banks of the Nile. Crown, pectoral, sandals of antelope hide he thrust in a cedar chest, and barefoot in a tattered loincloth, a weathered bag at his side, he tiptoed between the twin sphinxes of the palace gates, out of royalty and into reality; out of a palace and into the rank and enthralling town of Chemmis, his second capital.

Gently asway athwart its floating island, green with a thousand palms, black with the burnt and forsaken fires of the poor, Chemmis was both a wonder and an embarrassment. Diorite obelisks seemed to touch the sky; acacias uplifted leafy screens around the villas of the rich, the courtier, the builder, the priest. Temples reëchoed to the dance of priestesses, white whirling flames among the holy fires, zither, sistrum, and flute made of music a sacrifice sweeter than ibex or antelope. Hathor, goddess of love, had wrought with supple hands. But jealous Set had scattered squalor and dirt before his exile to the forbidden South. Temple walls, encrusted with shacks like milky skin with wounds, shamed both gods and men. Canvas stalls, folded against the night, reeked of the day's transactions, fish and sheep, entrails, scales and manure. Slaves from Nubia, source of men and gold, carried burdens to strain an ass's back. Ancient women, withered in robes which resembled winding sheets, proffered gems and girls to scribes and lords, farmers and river men. Perfume and putrefaction; splendor and squalor. In a word, Egypt.

Why had a crowd assembled in front of the temple to Bast? Of course! An animal fight to honor the goddess of cats. In a wicker cage, a basilisk fought a cobra. It was no longer true that the stare of a basilisk turned a cobra to stone (the truth had fled with magic to the South). The basilisk must fight like another snake with fang and tail. Bets were exchanged: a calf for three lambs, a week's catch of fish for a new net. Friends became rivals, exchanging the salty epithets of men who lived on the river, blessing or cursing the gods with the familiarity of a people at ease with their fate—Wazt, protectress of cobras; Min, lord of fertility; Hathor, lady of love; Anubis, guide to the dead. . . .

"A lamb for Wazt if the cobra wins!"

"May Min send you stunted dwarves instead of children!"

Pepy was tempted to linger and watch the fight. Truly it was a valiant basilisk. Half as large as the cobra, half as venomous, he needed cheers and deserved encouragement. But Pepy's bag was like a cornucopia: he must exhaust its riches before Harpocrates returned to Pharaoh.

First, a slight addition. He sidled against a carrying chair and loosened the anklet of a fat old matriarch, pink with carmine, perfumed with frankincense, so deftly that she seemed to mistake his touch for a fly and shook her foot without turning her head from the spectacle. (Ha! The basilisk's fangs were hooked in the cobra's neck.)

Another gift for the poor. Good. Under the canopy of a tamarisk tree slept Tike, the orphan boy who, much too proud to beg, lived by the fish he caught in the Nile and sold in the marketplace. Pepy had heard the songs with which he lured the fish to his line. Tike suffered a lowly station: fisherboy with no single possession except his flute. But the consummate artist showed in his supple hands and the softness of his speech, ungrammatical—he tended to drop his "h's"—but as musical as a lyre. He would never become a warrior; he would never become a builder; he was as evanescent as a moonbeam—and as unforgettable. As a rule, Pepy liked doers better than dreamers; he did not know why he had chosen Tike for special gifts; only that artistry in the boy seemed a kind of aristocracy beyond his understanding but not beyond his respect.

Pepy examined the anklet in the light of flickering

rushes—gold inlaid with peridots like round liquid
flames—a rare and costly piece as old as the first
mastaba, a month of meals for a boy, and prepared to
bestow his gift. Tike, however, did not wear a
garment in which to conceal the anklet from profes-
sional thieves or drunken boatmen. Naked like many
peasant boys, he was as thin as a reed in the Delta
marshes, but healthily brown from the sun and as
clean as Pepy after a bath.

Gently he shook the boy into consciousness, feeling
familiar, feeling paternal (as once his father had
shaken him).

"Here," he said. "Sell it for food."

Then he was gone, as swift as an oryx pursued by
hunters.

"'Arpocrates!" cried Tike with the desperation of
an awakening sleeper who strains to recapture a dream.

Wistfully Pepy looked behind him, wishing, wishing . . . what? To join the fisherboy on the riverbank
and play the flute or cast a net or build a bark of
papyrus reeds? To work when he needed food, but
mostly to play; mostly be his age? No! He was Pepy
II. Harpocrates. Both had been born to duty. Judgment. Justice. Let fisherboys like Tike dream by the
river; *he* would protect them; *he* would feed them.
(Still, he wished for his father to help him; to guide
the boy who was lost between child and pharaoh.)

It was almost time for Ra to skim above the horizon
in his bark or chariot and drive the mists from the
many-islanded Delta. Harpocrates must return to the
palace and reassume his royalty. He had emptied his
bag of a silver armlet, an anklet of gold, a pectoral
of lapis lazuli, and other palace treasures which would
feed the poor instead of awe ambassadors or rust in
tombs. If Henna missed them, well, he would fabricate
a story about nocturnal thieves. He was good at fabri-

cations. Was he not Harpocrates, his own creation?

He was also a tired little boy who wanted his bed. He dreamed of dancing dwarves.

Pepy lay on a warm limestone slab beside a steaming pool in the bath of his second palace. Memphis, of course, was his formal capital; Memphis held larger palaces, baths, and tombs; mummies of dogs and crocodiles as well as of men; but Chemmis had been his father's favorite island; and Chemmis belonged to Harpocrates. A Nubian slave, smooth and tough as the trunk of a palm tree but sweet of voice as the wind in the fronds, scrubbed his back with a pumice stone. Pepy had ruled the Twin Kingdoms for six years. The prospect of two baths a day, the pumice, the palm oil, for the rest of his earthly incarnation was only less disagreeable to him than the fact that he must eventually marry his sister, to say nothing of assorted cousins and foreign princesses. He did not dislike women; he had worshipped his mother whom he had lost to the Black Sleep; he detested, however, the notion of marriage to Henna and the expectation that he must share a bed with her and discuss the shape of wigs or the duties of palace menials when he would rather hunt the Bedouins who had mortally wounded his father or join Harkhuf, his caravan leader, and search the jungles of Yam for a dancing dwarf.

"Jacinth," he said, "if you scrub any more, I'll look like a leper. I was already clean when you started. Now I'm skinned."

Jacinth laughed, and his laughter rang as silkenly as the wind chimes, shaped like parakeets, which the Nubians hung in their trees.

"Pharaoh must set an example. He must be not only clean, he must be the cleanest."

"In your country, does everyone take a bath?"

Jacinth shrugged. "Baths are for pharaohs. Wash off the oil of the body and put on the oil of the coconut." In his own country, he had been a powerful prince; he had become an obedient slave with the good-humored resignation which characterized his hand-some, semi-barbarous people, who could turn a com-pliment like an Egyptian courtier and twist a knife like a dreaded Black Dwarf. In fact, the Nubians were often compared to palm trees, which often bent but rarely broke; whose fronds were lush to the eye but sharp to the finger; whose wood could be fashioned into a bed or a chair or cut into deadly slivers for a spear or dart.

"Wash off oil, put on oil. I end up just where I started. Except now I smell like a whore. Do you know, Jacinth, I would like to live in Nubia."

"What does my young master know of whores?" smiled Jacinth, looking like one who has heard a secret and hopes to be wheedled into a confession.

"Oh, everything," said Pepy, who actually knew nothing except that he liked whores better than Henna and the ladies of her court. The word to describe them was *more:* livelier laughter, larger breasts, lips like split pomegranates. The very look of them, their sidling glances, their undulating walk, fascinated him. Unlike Henna, they looked both giving and forgiving; they looked like women instead of men with wigs. He did, however, dislike the overabundance of nard with which they doused their bodies. At least he could say for Henna that she smelled like leather instead of perfume.

Before his slave could probe his ignorance, he hur-ried to ask, "Do you know, Jacinth, if I couldn't live in Nubia, I might choose Yam."

Nubia, a country of granite and deserts, lay to the south of Egypt; Yam, a country of jungles, dwarves,

and demons, lay to the south of Nubia. Pepy had read
his father's warning—read it, memorized it, preserved it
in a casket of porphyry—but twelve-year-old pharaohs
are not always as obedient as they are loving. The
letter, in fact, intrigued him with Yam. A demon of
fever had killed his father's father and fled to the
South. Why, then it should be pursued, it, and the
sta and the sphinx and the . . . but his thoughts were
turning heretical. To Pepy, pursuit did not always
mean punishment.

"Monkeys and Minikins and—"

"Crocodiles. Cobras. Hippopotami."

"We have those here. I could put up with a few
more if I hadn't to bathe so often. Besides, if I went
to Yam, Harkhuf would guide me." Harkhuf, a nobleman from the island of Elephantine, had been a friend
to the late Pepy I, a confidant to his son. He had recently left his villa to lead an expedition in search of
gold and apes, ivory and slaves, and, at Pharaoh's
special command, a *dancing dwarf.* Just as the young
noblemen of other countries led armies, so those of
Egypt, whose aspirations were more mercantile than
military and who were protected by pathless deserts
from sudden invasion, found their adventure by leading expeditions into untraveled regions and returning
with slaves—and assorted treasures to please the Pharaoh and bedizen his ladies. The Egyptians never enslaved their own people, though they sometimes fed
them to crocodiles.

Jacinth fingered the scarab at his throat. "You"—he
sometimes forgot to address his Pharaoh by title but
quickly caught his mistake and resumed, "My esteemed
master has not encountered the Green Melancholy."

"I've had the black kind. When my faher died." His
father had been the measure of love for him and
stretched his heart, so it seemed, to the size of a

coconut. "And it still jumps out at me when I'm not expecting it. Like something behind the door. What makes the green different?" (His mother had died before he had memorized her face, but his black melancholy often expanded, like the inky cloud of a squid, to include her along with his father, a god and goddess with open arms.)

"Does my master hold audience today?" Jacinth asked, sidestepping the question with a winsome smile which, however, did not deceive Pepy. There was fear behind the smile.

"Yes," sighed Pepy, hearing distantly from the city streets the laughter of children at play (knucklebones? leapfrog?); knowing that he must listen attentively to their parents' complaints, promise bounties, give commands, but that the bounties would only be bestowed at Henna's command, and Henna at twenty was not a bountiful sister. He was not afraid of her. He was not in the least afraid of crowds or foreign ambassadors or even kings, but he disliked pretending a power which did not exist and making promises which he could not keep. Today's audience threatened a multitude of problems. He did not need any spies to tell him that there was a restlessness in the land, a nameless discontent, a shapeless fear. Farmers haggled for prices with more malice than humor. Fishermen and butchers cheated instead of bargained; courtiers and ladies exchanged insults instead of compliments. The scales of Osiris trembled toward the night. And he, Pharaoh, must try to console for what he could not understand; combat a melancholy which did not even have a color. Fittingly, it was the Year of the Crocodile.

He rose from the slab, disgustingly clean, red if not raw, and submitted to a vigorous toweling from Jacinth, then the application of an oil so pungent that he wished for a second toweling. There was a time when, a child of six, he had lain beside his father, the Pharaoh, in the same bath, massaged by the same Nubian, and listened to talk of voyaging to Punt and building canals and "loving a woman as pretty and frail as a blue centaurea, your dead mother. Pepy, remember the gods and give them their due sacrifice of bullocks and sheep, milk and wine, but remember that you too are a god, and fear neither man nor demon and disgrace no woman."

"Please, Father," he had protested, trying to be a man at six, trying to be his father's son, but wanting to cry like a little girl, "you sound like you were going away."

"If I go, it will be to join Ra in his golden bark."

"I don't care about the gold," he had shouted. "It's still a going."

"Going is coming, my son."

His father had died in a minor skirmish with a tribe of Bedouins, who had taken to raiding Egyptian farms. . . .

"Pepy."

"Yes, Father?"

"It is I, Jacinth, your servant. I had meant to say 'My lord.'"

"Never mind, Jacinth. In your own land, *you* were a lord."

"My own land—that is what I mean to speak about. And Yam to the South."

"Speak then, Jacinth."

"My lord may never visit them. Unless—"

"Jacinth, what do you mean? Is it my red hair?" Red was the luckless color, the color of demons. Pharaohs were meant to be dark like Pepy I, whose hair had been as black as obsidian.

"There are those who would like to see Pharaoh

dead. They would rather worship his mummy than his presence."

"But why, Jacinth? I haven't any power. You know that!"

"Ah, but power is starting to come. There are those who have seen him leave the palace as Harpocrates and do the work of a man. Gatekeepers and others."

"The gatekeeper is my friend."

"Gold is also a friend."

"And the others?"

"Has my lord enjoyed his bath?"

Chapter II

_____

Harkhuf had left his men in the open, grassy veldt, in their tents of black goatskin, commanded by his Nubian officer, Dedwen. Safety lay in the veldt, where the white-barked acacias were closer to bushes than trees and a keen-eyed watchman could sight a rhinoceros before he could catch the man's scent. As for lions, they skulked and lurked and happened upon you even in the veldt, but what was a predatory lion compared to the Black Dwarves, who carved their arrowheads out of human bones? Or the sphinxes whose lashing tails were as cruel as a slaver's whip? Or the sly little Minikins with their skull-shattering boomerangs? Safety, a plump and familiar wife, languished among the tents. Adventure, a hot-tempered whore, frolicked and wantoned in the jungle.

Now he was unencumbered and blissful in solitude. No servile retainers to gather around him like a gaggle of geese: "My lord, shall I fetch you a wig for the coming festival?" "My lord, you have broken a strap on your left ankle. . . ." No female admirers to honk in his ear, particularly wives, particularly a wife by the name of Ti, the princess from Babylon. (In truth, he had _tried_ to save her from the crocodiles. He had even tried to collect her remains and recovered a large amethyst ring, apparently indigestible, though needing a jewelsmith to restore the polish and smooth the chips. Dutifully he had raised a small pyramid in her honor and enclosed her things—the amulet, the anklets, the wigs—seventeen of them, ranging from saffron to umber, from beehives to hornet nests—all of the gee-gaws which had delighted her brittle foreign heart—and sent her soul on its way to the Celestial Ladder.)

But now he was happily wifeless in the jungles of Yam. He scarcely knew the names of the trees. Banyan, banana, baobab with shady leaves instead of the leafless branches which languished in drier climates. . . . But why must a tree be named and described and compared? The floor of the jungle was more of a slush than a ground, for he was close to the ubiquitous Nile. But he did not mind a squishing beneath his feet with such arboreal wonder above his head. I have entered a sun temple grown by the gods, he thought. The trees are its lotus-tipped columns, the vines which tangle their nethermost limbs are the roof, and the filtered light of Ra's chariot shines to me as if through clerestory windows.

Perhaps in just such a temple he would find his dwarf, his gift for the little friend who happened also to be his Pharaoh. Thus had Pepy written:

"And you must bring with you this dwarf, alive, sound and well, from the land of spirits, for the dance of the god, and to rejoice and gladden the heart of the King of Upper and Lower Egypt. . . . When he comes down with you into the vessel, appoint trust-worthy people who shall be beside him on either side of the vessel; take care lest he should fall into the water. When he sleeps at night, appoint trustworthy people who shall sleep beside him in his tent; inspect ten times a night. For I desire to see this dwarf more than the products of Sinai and Punt. . . ."

Ah, the squish of his feet in the slush! Ah, the

vegetal scent of the air! And the birds . . . surely this was the Paradise for birds. Starlings with wings like somber flames . . . ebony ibises with beaks like curved Bedouin knives. . . . And what were those tiny black creatures which perched in the bushes and fluttered their roseate feathers to catch the moisture which dripped from the trees?

And what was the sound . . . song . . . summons which seemed to speak in his mind: "Come, come, come"?

It was thus that he came to the Curiosity.

At first he did not recognize its nature. Does a man, ignorant of sphinxes, recognize all of those seemingly dissimilar parts—man's head, lion's haunches, bennu's wings, Isis only knew what kind of tail—as belonging to the same beast? This too seemed many disparate parts: vegetable, however, not animal. Gradually he saw that they belonged to the same plant: stem as thick as the trunk of an ancient cedar; leaves so large that one of them would thatch a peasant's hut; and petals, by Hathor's breast, the petals lifted and swirled into a flower like a monumental goblet. Curiously, the petals were green like the leaves, though heavier, gemlike to the eye. What demon or deity drank from such a cup?

It was a green miracle. It was a green mystery. Well, this was Yam, this was the land for miracles and mysteries.

Having discovered a lotus the size of a tree, he was not unprepared for a ladder trailing down the stem, its vines interwoven to fit a human foot. Any man with a sense of adventure would want to climb such a ladder and explore the flower (and answer the song, "Come, come, come. . . .").

His big feet threatened to snap the rungs. He was

a trim and sinewy, not a burly, man, but his feet were big for his height. Still, the rungs supported him even if they drooped, the ladder swayed and dipped but did not spill him onto the ground, and soon he was climbing among the smooth and tapered leaves.

He might have been entering a little jungle removed and remote from the jungle under him! There was a fragrance about the place, a sweet acridity of stem and rainswept leaves and alien greennesses which he did not try to name. I have been led to this flower, he thought. I have been led to greet—a plant?—a goddess?—a monster?

He emerged from the leaves to confront the bloom. Impervious it looked. A puzzlement of tightly packed petals. He was not, however, surprised to find a door, as neatly cut as a rockcutter's oval into the side of a cliff. He was only surprised at his momentary doubt. Stooping, he entered the flower.

No longer was he trodding on vegetation. Behold! A path of round olivine stepping-stones. Truly a sacred place. He felt the urge to advance, explore, possess. If he ever attained the Celestial Paradise, a doubtful prospect at best, he would probably elude the judging deities and hurry into the presence of the unapproachable Ra and demand a seat reserved for pharaohs in the solar chariot.

He blinked his eyes to see in the misty green light . . . a roof of petals bent into a dome; walls like the roof, green, hard, gemlike, a temple beyond price; floor embedded with rainbow-colored molluscs from the Nile and pathed with the olivines on which he stood. Temple? Somehow it seemed a house. The furnishings were few but familiar: a brazier shaped like a hippopotamus and burning amberly in the green light . . . a table with feet like the tails of crocodiles . . . and a bed so large that he thought of orgies instead of couples. The bed fascinated him (beds always fascinated him). It was a wide expanse of silken softnesses raised on wooden tails like those of—yes, again—crocodiles. He rather liked the choice of tail.

A smaller bed, like a baby whale with its mother, companioned the immensity; an empty cradle in fact, a hollowed tortoiseshell with swaddling clothes; and toys were scattered over the floor, a harp in the shape of a bent baboon, the strings taut between the tail and head, a boat of meru wood with a shimmering sail.

He walked toward the bed. Whatever hit him was like an invisible kick from an ass. He doubled with pain and fell to the floor, gasping for breath to curse the deity of the place, the demon, the ka. . . . No, it was worse than a kick; a rabid ichneumon seemed to gnaw at his vitals.

He wanted to die. For the first time in his life, this bold warrior, this tireless adventurer, this indefatigable warrior who had never lost a fight, wanted to die. Suddenly a possible answer came to him. The ka or spirit of Ti had not remained in her pyramid or ascended the Celestial Ladder. True to her Babylonian temperament (temper for short), she had somehow come to Yam, the country of demons, and claimed this particular flower for her mischief. Now she was punishing him. Invariably they had fought their worst arguments in bed. Thus the bed, with crocodile feet to reproach him for her demise. She had wanted a child to "enrich your line with a bit of Babylonian royal." He had tersely refused her request and laced her wine with the juice of Love-Me-Not, the flower of infertility. "Pepy is already like a son to me," he had said, "and as for a daughter, she would only get herself with child by a household slave and bring shame on both of us." Thus the cradle and toys to reproach him. Hathor, what a revengeful woman!

"Ti," he shouted (the shout resounded from petaled wall to wall, like the cry of a lonely ka). "I *didn't* shove you out of the boat. I didn't even *rock* the boat. Truly! And I tried my best to beat off the crocodiles."

Ti remained inscrutable. The pain redoubled instead of diminished. His vitals were gone; the emptiness hurt him more than the feast.

"And I tried to collect your remains to mummify. I managed to save your amethyst"—he wore it now on his own finger—"and I built you a pyramid. Pink. Your favorite color."

Inscrutable. Implacable.

"No!"

He gave a tremendous cry.

Protest. Denial. Defiance.

"NO!"

The cry was at once his weapon and his retreat, backwards, bent like a sapling in a sirocco, out of the room and down the ladder, and into the slush (harder earth would have killed him). Pain on his track like a swift-footed lion, he raced for his camp and friends.

"Curse her," he muttered under his breath. "May six hippopotami sit on her soul."

Her or it?

The Nubians spoke of the Green Melancholy. Perhaps he was wrong to blame his deceased wife.

"Curse them," he muttered. "Both of them."

"By Hathor's udder!" he grinned, swallowing beer from a hollow papyrus stem and relishing the crudities of his tent, the goatskin walls which admitted the cacophonies of the night but not the emanations of a vengeful lotus—marmoset cry, leopard roar, elephant trumpet—the straw pallet, the wicker basket of wild bananas, the absence of furniture, elegant friends in elaborate wigs, and, wonder of wonders, *wife* (may she rot in her flower).

Tomorrow, he thought, I will look for dancing dwarves. Tomorrow but not tonight. I ought to have been a Bedouin. Wander by day with my herds from oasis to oasis and fight an occasional battle—victorious of course—for a choice water hole, a shade of coconut palms. Take my pleasure at night with wine and women. Not *woman*. Ti had presumed to limit his dalliances; he, Harkhuf, a nobleman of Egypt! He could have supported a dozen legal wives, including spendthrift princesses, a limitless choice of concubines and, being a man who preferred cheap beer to rare wine, an occasional raunchy, free-living, loud-swearing whore. What did he get? A *single* wife, and one who had sighed at the age of fourteen on their wedding night, "Dearest boy, I mean no disrespect when I say that love is better in poems than in bed. You have mussed my hair—I shall never get it untangled—and will you kindly return my robe? The night air will give me a chill."

"What did you expect?" he asked. After all at fourteen he was not without experience—rustic girls, housemaids, even a young priestess of Hathor.

"Tenderness," she had said with the ignorance of youth. "My robe, if you please."

In eleven years, she had matured into a woman who, like the glittering waters of the Great Green Sea, promised to quench your thirst; but taste her and you tasted brine.

Well, crocodiles had their uses.

Then he heard the sound. A quick, whooshing whistle, like a large insect or a small bird. Of course. A boomerang. Of course. The Minikins. He had never seen a Minikin in the flesh—but the Nubians, venturing into these southern regions for the long-necked giraffes whose tails they sold to Egyptian lords for fly-whisks and the elephants whose tusks were carved by Egyptian artisans into furniture and jewelry, had described the diminutive race in precise and awed details. Shy little beings, dangerous too, brown as a rare palm wine, they lived in houseboats which they rowed from lake to river, river to rivulet, to baffle their enemies, the redoubtable Black Dwarves. They moved with the speed of gazelles, and you never suspected their presence until you heard their boomerangs which, if they did not lodge in your skull, returned to their throwers for another journey.

For Harkhuf, to think was to act. Bow in hand, he leaped from the tent to shout commands; to gather his men, dusky Nubians and brown Egyptians. He ducked as a boomerang whistled over his head, raised his bow and sent an arrow into a quivering thicket of grasses, silver and streaming in the light of the youthful Khonsu, whose chariot moon gleamed lordlier in the tropics than in the North. The grasses ceased to quiver; Harkhuf, warily investigating, discovered a small prostrate form with a large arrow treelike in his breast. Until he examined the corpse, he felt as if he had killed a child. Instead of a Minikin, he found a Black Dwarf, a squat and misshapen being with knock knees and distended belly and skin the color of dark volcanic tufa. Naked except for a tuft of feathers at his rump, he might have been sired by an ostrich on a pig.

Nevertheless, they moved like eddies of wind in the elephant grass with its bamboo-thick stems and its broad leaves, among the tree-heath, treacherous with thorns. You had to guess their direction and shoot ahead of them. At the same time, you must duck and twist to avoid their boomerangs. Rarely you glimpsed

their features, black, vicious, intent upon killing as
well as defending. What did they need to defend, these
creatures out of the jungle strayed into the veldt?

Harkhuf's men were accustomed to fighting by
night; they had fought the Bedouins. Bare of chest,
lithe in their knee-length loincloths, bending their
bows and their heads at the same time, they vastly
outnumbered the eddies; hushed them with persistent
twang of bowstrings and the whisk of arrows. The
camp resounded like a hive of enormous bees, preparing for frost. (Reason conquering magic? He did not
like the comparison. *Egyptians defending their camps
against barbarians.*)

In spite of surprise and boomerangs and the unfamiliar terrain, the attack was brief, the end inevitable.
For Harkhuf commanded fifty skilled bowmen.
Twelve little bodies, three of them women, littered
the environs of the camp.

He had lost only two of his men, Nubians both of
them. Only? Nubian? They had been his friends, his
fellow wanderers under the Seven Imperishable Stars.
He would bury them in their sandals, standing and
facing Nubia to ease the return of their kas to their
homeland and thence to whatever region awaited such
lesser folk.

Now to the wounded. Some were in pain. Harkhuf
knew the proper conjurations; more important, the
herb for parted flesh (the woody nightshade), the
means to bind a wound or set a broken limb. After a
recent battle with the Bedouins, he had even trepanned
a skull to relieve the pressure against a bowman's brain.
Medicine was a combination of prayers to invoke the
gods and frighten evil spirits—those who had lingered
in Egypt after the Great Exorcism—and of practical
measures to help the helpers and hinder the harmers.
He chanted an ancient jingle, childish but efficacious

because, for the most part, demons resembled children, mischievous and often cruel yet easily frightened:

> Demon, get thee from my friend,
> Lest a crocodile shall rend,
> Lumpish hippopotamus
> Roll upon his back and squash
> Presence demoniacal,
> Devilment invisible.

"Dedwen," he said to a young Nubian officer, his first in command. "I see you're hiding a wound. Come, I will bind it for you."

"I am honored that Harkhuf, my lord, should tend his devoted servant."

"Officer, not servant." He disliked servility except among women. "Am I hurting you, Dedwen?"

The Nubian smiled and shrugged. "At the age of seven, your people made me a slave—I who had been a nobleman in my own land. But it was you who set me free. How could you hurt me, Harkhuf, my friend and my lord?"

"Pain is no respecter of friendship."

"Well, then, you are hurting me for the moment but easing me for the future. It is quite likely that you are saving my life. But Harkhuf. The Black Dwarves belong to the jungle. Why did they come into the veldt?" Dedwen liked an answer to every question: why did the gods pour torrential rains upon Yam but scarcely a sprinkle upon Egypt? Why did the women of Knossos bare their breasts but not their thighs? Why was Dedwen black and Harkhuf brown? Harkhuf had journeyed into Yam to search for intriguing questions; Dedwen had followed him to find satisfying answers. He looked as purposeful as one of those slim hunting dogs with pointed ears, poised to flush a goose from a clump of papyrus stalks. "We weren't threatening them. They couldn't know you meant to capture a child to send Pharaoh. They always build their houses in kapok trees."

"Perhaps an acacia tree," suggested Harkhuf.

"Too small even for dwarves." He had not been given a proper reason; the goose still eluded him.

"This may be a sacred place. An underground temple or such. If you build underground, the jungle is not your place. The soil is much too damp. You must seek a desert or veldt."

"Then there may be more of them under us now?"

"When they fight, they all fight together," said Harkhuf. "And die together, even the women, as we have seen. But there may be children." He thought of his dancing dwarf for Pepy, a *young* dwarf, agile, able to learn, not yet distorted into maturity. He parted the grasses with the end of his bow.

"All right now, men. Help me look." He had not yet lost his fascination for doors, in spite of lethal lotuses; sometimes they led to magic.

Such doors were the reason for Harkhuf's explorations; indeed, his life. Such doors were shut in the North where the priests no longer conjured and cursed and danced to attain a bountiful harvest, a beautiful wife, a strong son. If Pepy I had driven Set from the land, the tail-lashing sphinxes, the stas more deadly than cobras, he had also exorcised erotic apparitions, will-o'-the-wisps, kindly sphinxes, in a word magic. Not in the rational North could you root for dwarves among the elephant grass. Not among pyramids, those monuments of architectural precision; or temples, built to endure the savage sands, the scorching sirocco winds, and rival eternity. In the South, magic was Pharaoh and no one threatened his sway.

His heart leaped in his breast like a netted carp.

There . . . there . . . the trodden grass . . . the deepest darkness in the light of a fugitive moon. Something awaited. . . .

The entranceway was smooth but narrow; he had to writhe and wriggle like a temple snake. Earth-scent, root-scent, dwarf-scent (feathers and blood and human excrement). Presences, intimations, lingerings . . . the sacredness of a shrine, the hush of a tomb. He, the invader; where, the defenders? Size was encumbrance. He wished himself dwindled, invisible, an eddy of wind in a region transgressed but not encompassed; as irresistible as a coral cave in the Deep Green Sea; as inexplicable as the flight of the solar chariot.

The broadening into several passageways, recently smoothed and bricked; then, the ladder of ivory rungs; then, the glory of flickering rushlights making a day of dusk.

"A *Minikin* temple," he said.

"How do you know?" asked practical Dedwen.

"The dwarves like ugliness."

The pink limestone walls had been smoothed and surfaced with careful hands. The floor, a mosaic of stones, enacted the Nile in miniature, its various creatures delighting in festival, smallest mollusc to largest crocodile. A frog cavorted aboard a lotus leaf. Beneficent Oxyrhynchids or spider-crabs, usually malignant, enwreathed the snout of a hippopotamus. Artists at one with the country had set the stones into scenes which portrayed a river which did not drown, animals which did not rend, nature without cruelty.

"And the furniture," said Harkhuf. "It looks as if it were made for a man instead of a mummy."

After the straight, stiff chairs of Egypt, the rounded chairs of lianas dried and dyed to a forest green and woven into backs and seats and cushioned with round cushions softer than those of Pharaoh's sister's bed-chamber, bedazzled his eyes and enticed his tired limbs. What was the soft and glistening cloth which enclosed those enticing roundnesses? (In the East, the remote, the unapproachable East beyond Arabia, there were said to be little worms which lived in mulberry trees and wove cocoons out of silver filaments which maidens in turn collected and wove into cloth called silk.)

"And the god of the place—"

An elephant with eight arms, benign of countenance, broad of trunk, sat in a magisterial limestone atop a pedestal like a throne. Being small, the Minikins worshipped size. They had set their offerings in front of the god—melons and baskets of flowers, rings and armbands and bracelets to rival the riches in a pharaoh's tomb.

"And gold," said Dedwen.

He might have said "Ra." Indeed, it was the god's own metal, believed to have formed in the earth when he had descended from heaven to walk among men, in the time before scribes had knelt to record history on the papyrus scrolls they held in their laps. The Egyptians mined the desert and even dug pools or basins along the Nile for panning the nuggets during the inundation.

"*Spun* gold," said Harkhuf, evaluating a heap to the side of the room, to the side of the stairs, apart not only in its position but in its difference. "It isn't hard, it isn't metal or stone. It seems to be cloth and—"

"My name is Immortelle."

The gold gathered itself into a girl; no, a young woman, small to be sure, but womanly in her poise and grace and smile.

Gold was the shimmering gown which fell from her shoulders and fluttered above her ankles; upswept hair to rival the crest of a phoenix; tiara encrusted with

liquid peridots. Gold, enwreathing a cluster of blue
stone stars in a pendant around her neck; golden, the
twin gazelles entwined around each arm. And the face,
the form! They needed no ornaments but, adorned
with many, managed not to be overwhelmed; managed to draw attention first to themselves and only
then the adornments.

In the light of the rushlamps, her hair was aflame
with gold—temple fire, holy fire, goddess fire. And
the bare arms—gold becoming alabaster; and the
infinitesimal feet less shod in than graced by sandals
with a single strap—they hardly seemed to have
touched the coarse, hard earth; perhaps they had flickered in eiderdown.

As for the face, well, if you could chisel wonder
into features. . . . The eyes were wonderful and also
slightly disconcerting. Lapis lazuli eyes; child's eyes,
looking upon the Great Green Sea for the first time,
observing a friendly sphinx, watching a phoenix build
her nest. The lips and the cheeks did not owe their
pink to any cosmetic palette; did they come from the
Celestial Garden? Even the characteristics of the race
—four toes instead of five; soft, downy, pointed ears
no larger than an acorn; horns like mother of pearl;
intimations that a gazelle, in the time before Egypt
numbered her dynasties, had sired them on a mortal
maiden—were wonderments instead of oddities.

"Who—who are you?" blurted the usually eloquent
Harkhuf. The unblinking eyes stared him into a
stammer.

Deftly she lifted her star-encrusted pendant and
rubbed it across her tongue. Harkhuf remembered the
practice, forbidden in Egypt, of evoking the secret
properties of a gem with the help of the tongue, a
member more sensitive than any fingertip, an exten-
sion, as it were, of the brain.

"Immortelle," she said in a voice as soft as the wind as he tiptoes through a courtyard or temple garden.

"The gem makes you able to understand me?"

"I could understand most of your words anyway. The Brown Minikins taught me. But to speak it—yes, the gem helps me."

"It is magic?"

She laughed. "To you perhaps. To me it is as dear and familiar as an old friend."

"You aren't from *here*," he said.

"No."

"Where then? Above?" Ra-gold; Ra's daughter, perhaps?

"Sappharine."

"The island in the Arabian Sea. Nobody goes there."

He was the greatest explorer in Egypt; he had braved the cataracts of the Nile; he had crossed deserts where vipers died of thirst; he had ventured into Yam; but even he had never dared that mysterious island named for a blue gem (the one in her star-shaped pendant?). "We have heard," he said, "that your shallows clash with rocks. That slimy dragons lumber out of the depths to smash a ship with a single lash of a tail. No one has ever returned from Sappharine. It is doubtful if any has even reached your shore."

"But I came from there on the back of a roc."

"Rock? I knew they clashed but I didn't know they flew."

"The bird, I mean. Tutu beside me on another bird. We flew here to Yam, Tutu and I, to pay our kinsmen a visit. Now he is dead."

He watched a single tear descend her cheek, swift, silver, evanescent. A falling star, he thought.

"I am a Golden Minikin, you see. In the time of your first pharaoh, my ancestors migrated here from Sappharine and grew brown with the tropic sun."

"Ra's sun doesn't give heat," he corrected her. "Only light."

"Well, perhaps they turned brown from their diet," she smiled. "We traveled, Tutu and I, from city to city on the backs of ostriches, led by gazelles, guarded by Minikin warriors riding oryxes. Everywhere we exchanged and received gifts. Here in this temple to Ganesh, the elephant god, we paused to give thanks for a safe and comfortable journey. Alas, he has lost his power in these parts. The dwarves had followed us from the jungle. They fell upon us like spiders, infested our temple, stole our boomerangs, killed and ate our animals and our escort. And Tutu."

He reached out a steadying hand and felt her sway like a crocus in the wind.

"What was he like, this Tutu you mention so often?" He felt an unaccountable jealousy, an indefensible pleasure in the death of a man he had never met.

"Not like you at all," she said. It was neither an insult nor a compliment. It was a simple statement of truth.

"Ah," sighed Harkhuf, feeling merest peasant in the presence of royalty. "It's true that my father tilled a field beside the Nile. But his back was straight and his arm was strong, and Pharaoh chose him for his personal guard. He became a lord. I became the friend of Pharaoh's son and then his little grandson, who now rules Egypt."

"Those who till the fields revere the gods," she said. "I did not intend to demean your origins. I only meant that Tutu was small and kind, easily broken, and you are large and strong, and hard, I think, to kill. I did not mean to call you less or more. Only different. Poor Tutu. He could have used the difference."

"Then I came," sighed Harkhuf.

"Yes. And you pitched your tents above dwarves and the temple. Up the ladder they clambered to drive you away, but you killed them with your tremendous bows. I climbed after them to make my escape. But an arrow grazed my head." She turned her cheek to him and Harkhuf saw her wound. "And I lost my senses and stumbled down the ladder."

"Dedwen will bring you a healing herb."

"A scratch, no more. I have deeper wounds."

"Of course," he said. "They violated you. That's why they kept you alive."

"Oh no. They didn't even try."

"Then they must have taken you for a goddess. The gold of you, the magic—everyone prizes gold. And to Black Dwarves, ugly and shapeless why, they must have worshipped you."

"Worshipped?" she cried. "They thought me hideous. They thought the sun had bleached me as it does the human bones they wear in their noses."

"Hideous?"

"They thought me so ugly that they molded clay images of me to frighten away demons. *That's* why they kept me alive. I was a—what do you call those images you put in your fields to drive away the birds?"

"Sphinx-terrors."

"I was a sort of sphinx-terror."

Mute corroboration, a table lay heaped with fresh clay, and molded clay in the shape of attenuated girls waving skinny arms. The molding was clumsy but the model was obvious.

"And now, I expect, you will make me a slave, though not for the same reason."

"Enslave a *queen?*"

"Oh, I am not a queen."

"Well then, a great lady, wed to a noble lord before he died. Ambassador as it were from a distant land."

"I am not a great lady and neither wed nor a widow." She gave, however, a regal smile, as if she were going to announce a loftier station, perhaps divinity.

"What then—" A goddess in truth, he thought, wondering if he should kneel or lift his arms in prayer.

"I am—how do you say?—one who pleases."

"A dancer? A singer?" he asked with increasing bewilderment. She was far too refined to be a dancing girl.

"Oh yes, both of those, of course. But I am not so limited in my skills." The blue eyes did not lose their innocence; at the same time, the shape of her body hinted minute perfections through her diaphanous robe. Breasts like the Apples of Love. Nipples redder than jasper and winking twin temptations through the cloth.

"Like all of my race I am, I believe, what you call a—" and she spoke the word with infinite pride, as one says "priestess" or "princess" or "Pharaoh's first wife"—

"WHORE."

Chapter III

In a courtyard blue with lotuses, in a palace with lotus-shaped columns bluer than the bluest flower, Pepy sat on his throne, an armless chair of sandstone and porphyry with feet like the paws of a lion, and granted audience to his restless people. The red crown of the North, like a bowl uprearing an ominous cobra hood, rested hotly upon his hot clinging wig. His pectoral, an intricacy of golden falcons inlaid with turquoise and carnelian, prickled his bare chest. He fixed his attention into an attitude of compassionate interest and, forgetting Henna beside him and the motley group assembled in front of him, wished for a father instead of a crown.

His hair, like a fire which was banked but unextinguished, flickered and coruscated through the coarse black strands of his official wig. Red as the Red Land. Red as the desert cliffs enkindled with noon. Everything about him suggested life, motion, energy constrained into the officialdom of Pharaoh; constrained but not compelled. The fires burned, the muscles rippled in his brown arms; the thrusting chest, incredible in a boy of twelve, threatened to burst his pectoral. Pepy as Pharaoh must honor the rituals of the five preceding dynasties (Pepy was Pharaoh and,

37

he hoped, would one day discard or create rituals to his pleasure).

"And he sold me pig meat instead of lamb," a woman complained as she pointed a fat accusatory finger at a young farmer. Pigs were lowly esteemed in Egypt. Evil spirits or kas processed their bodies and tainted their flesh. The woman reminded Pepy of a pelican—large stomach and gaping mouth. He would have liked to throw her a rancid fish. But the charge appeared to be true. He must mete a punishment, at least a fine.

"Sentence the rogue to eat a pregnant sow," whispered Henna.

"I sentence Khonsu, the fisherman, to make a public apology," he announced in a voice of surprising power for a child. It happened with every audience. The people expected to wheedle a little boy but found a budding pharaoh. Still, everyone knew that Henna was like a cactus flower already in bloom; her petals, dry and colorless, did not impress them, but they could not ignore her thorns.

The woman's jaw hung slack in the way of a pelican. (I ought to throw her a squid, thought Pepy.) The fisherman grinned with relief. Brown, brawny, dressed only in a pair of sandals and a scarab ring, he suggested the sun instead of the moon for whom he was named.

"Naked," scowled Henna, as if such splendid nudity could affront anyone except a Babylonian.

"Blessed be the pharaoh who metes such justice," said Khonsu. "I, a lowly fisherman, hereby acknowl-edge—" Then, forgetting his formal manners, he knelt and kissed Pepy's sandals.

"He has touched you," cried Henna to Pepy. "He has touched Pharaoh's flesh!"

Before she could order him thrown to the crocodiles a cry distracted the crowd. Someone might have cried "fire" or "flood" or "Bedouins."

"A phoenix!"

Then, the silence of disbelief. Then, the repetition. "*A phoenix!*"

Then, the conflagration.

"Approaching from the East."

"Arabia, where else?"

"Bigger than an eagle, and Ra, what claws!"

"And see the golden crest on her head!"

A wind devil might have stricken the garden. Lotuses snapped, palm trees bent, an audience had become a turbulence.

"Pigs," said Henna. "Pigs, all of them, gone to their slop." Cool, expressionless, looking more like a statue of copper hammered over wood than a young woman, she retained her throne. She restrained her brother by seizing his loincloth.

"But a *phoenix*," he protested. "We must welcome her to the temple of the Sun." Only twice in every millenium, at the start, again in five hundred years, was a phoenix expected to arrive from Arabia and build a nest in the temple. The arrival was auspicious and punctual, the building of the nest was celebrated by a reluctant fast and a riotous festival and, by the time the bird had perished and risen from her own ashes, most of Egypt was happily drunk on palm wine and barley beer, and assured of national prosperity until the next bird.

The last bird, strictly on schedule, had arrived, built, perished, risen, and departed *three hundred and seven years before the death of Pepy I.* The Egyptian calendar was unarguable; there was no mistaking the number of years (though every year must account for five extra days). Phoenixes whose arrival was unanticipated —gratuitous, they were called—augured invasion, plague, a pestilence of locusts to destroy the grain. . . . A victory, a bountiful harvest, the ascension of a great king. Change, perhaps for the better, perhaps for the worse, but *monumental*. The arrival of a phoenix in the reign of Pharaoh Narmer had augured a plague which had devastated the newly joined Kingdoms.

Removing his crown, Pepy delivered a stomp to his sister's foot; she relaxed her hold and gave him her basilisk stare.

"Sow," he shouted over his shoulder as he abdicated his throne and his dignity and followed the herd toward the temple which loomed like a sphinx at the edge of the Nile.

A fishwife jostled him, swore, recoiled in horror when she recognized Pharaoh without his crown. Peasants did not touch gods. She awaited a thunderbolt.

"Never mind," he consoled her. "I got in the way."

In the way. . . . How else to describe his rule? Everyone except Henna treated him with respect in spite of his years, a boy but also a king, a king but also a god. But he knew from the time of his ascension to the throne that it was Henna who really ruled the country. Egyptian women enjoyed equality with their men, and Princess Henna, though her breasts were as flat as barley cakes (and much less appetizing) and her scrubby red hair required a permanent wig (without the wig it was difficult to tell if she were a man or a woman), demanded autocracy. The fact that she was expected to become his wife did not increase her appeal. He would as soon have slept with a scrofulous cow, though the deeper implications of marriage, the full range of marital duties, were lost to him. Even as Harpocrates he supposed that beds were shared for nothing more complicated than warmth or convenience, and that babies descended from Hathor into a mother's womb. He knew the facts of the stars, the land, the river, the Great Green Sea, but the facts of life had been kept from him as carefully as the key to a mummy case from a doubtful guard.

He had always imagined the bird as a splendor of sunbright gold. It was gold and also gems. Gold for the crest; amethyst head and body flourishing into an aquamarine tail with garnet flickerings. An aerial pectoral (but only a goddess could carve such flawless jewels). Surely so rare a bird could not foreshadow evil. Why, she must be as large as the largest eagle, and how she cavorted and twinkled above the temple, that resplendent rectangle flanked by obelisks! Would she land on the flat roof in the expected way and build her nest of cassia twigs and frankincense?

No. She dipped a stately wing above the temple and then, like a pharaoh's queen disdaining his pyramid, poised above the Nile, august and unapproachable, and climbed toward her second home in the sun.

The sky resembled an ocean which has never known a storm; a halcyon sea without a nest; a sweetness compounded of wonder at remembering and sorrow at loss.

"Was 'e really a phoenix?" Tike asked of Pepy, failing to recognize Harpocrates without his umber hair; recognizing his Pharaoh but not in awe of *him*.

"Phoenixes are 'she.' Yes, she was real enough. The colors, the queenliness. But now she's gone."

"Then 'e didn't like us," said the fisherboy, looking as if he had lost the largest fish which had ever tugged his line.

"She."

"'E wouldn't bide long enough even to build 'is nest."

"I think," said Pepy, groping, "I think 'e—she—did like us. Perhaps she came to warn us."

"About what?" cried Tike, surprised. (A typical dreamer, thought Pepy. He thinks that a phoenix should come with gifts, not warnings. He thinks that poverty is another name for freedom, and the gift he would like would be a magic flute or a song to sing to his fish.)

"I don't know," said Pepy, stripping a golden bracelet from his wrist and pressing it into the startled boy's hand.

"About drought." A carrying chair of Lebanese cedar draped with varicolored leather and trailing crimson tassels. Attendant Nubians as black as the Nile in flood. Henna. She delivered the dire pronouncement as one might say, "Feed the hippopotamus."

Her list grew increasingly monotonous. Unfortunately, it was also ominous. "Crop failure. Starvation. This year the Nile will fail to properly flood. And next year and next. Three years of drought."

Her wig, which crouched atop her head like a bent cat, had tilted dangerously over her left ear. The galena with which she darkened her eyes had begun to streak in the sun. Wickedly Pepy wished for a bronze mirror to show her her unregality as she made her pronouncements. To be, as she liked to say, *unregal*, was to sin against nature's god-decreed design, the flow of the nurturing Nile, the daily course of Ra in his chariot sun.

"Oh, Henna, what do you know about phoenixes? It could mean prosperity. It could mean victory in battle." He rather liked the thought of a battle. An army of barbarous Bedouins from the West. . . . A horde of black barbarians from Punt. He, Pepy, leading the charge, bending his father's bow. The youngest general in Egypt's six dynasties. . . .

"I had a dream."

Pepy resigned himself to a lengthy explanation. Henna's dreams were as interminable as they were accurate.

She extended a hand which brandished a single golden feather; it looked like spun silk; it seemed to burn with its own interior light and it made her skin look coarse in comparison, a small weathered brazier holding a pure flame.

"But where—?"

"Out of the sky," she said, like a teacher addressing ignorant children in the use of the abacus or the mysteries of the calendar.

"And there's a second," cried Pepy.

"And a third," cried Tike. "Gifts?"

"Warnings." Henna did not arise from her chair. Languidly she signaled Tike to catch the second and third feathers and lay them, without touching her sacrosanct person, in her outstretched palm. Her voice was deep and oracular, as if it came from a cave in the rocky flanks of the Nile. (Merciful Ra, thought Pepy, she's in her pharaoh mood. Well, she's built for a king. Except for the vital appendage.)

"Exactly. For three straight years the Nile will fail to flood. Irrigate our fields. Fill our canals. For three straight years, hunger will stalk the land like a ravening crocodile."

"But what have we *done?*" cried Pepy. "Didn't our father build a temple to Ra?"

"It is not the sun we have dishonored. It is Father Nile himself, ancient of days, strong in wisdom, swift in judgment. Somehow we have despoiled him, tainted him, desecrated him. Were the cows not devoured on his banks?"

"What cows?" asked Tike.

"Those in my dream, urchin. Did the bird not dip above the river before he returned to the sun?"

"But why?" gasped Pepy.

"Ah," said Henna, inscrutable; inscrutability no doubt hiding inability to answer the ultimate question. "I do not presume to explain the wrath of a god. It is enough to predict and warn."

That night in his great canopied bed, that night when his room was redolent of cedar chests and meru-wood chairs, of palm scents, city scents, Nile scents issuing through the high, thin slits which served for windows, he heard a whispering like the crackle of spider legs in withered leaves.

Henna, his sister, and Ayub, the priest of Ra, had met in the garden, and certainly not for a tryst. They sounded—conspiratorial.

It was not a time to sleep. He crept from his bed, Harpocrates the Silent, and opened the lattice door.

Like a fetching whore, the courtyard offered her bounties to the moon. Palm trees and paths and pool of blue lotuses. Date palms, coconut palms, raffia palms like the giant quills of the roc, a fabulous bird from the East. Paths of crushed coquina shells. Pool of blue lotuses like goblets uplifted to catch the wine of the moon. Across the pool, he distinguished Henna's figure, wigless and masculine (Hathor had somehow forgotten to give her breasts), and with her Ayub, a young man misplaced as a priest, a young man, so he guessed, who would like to sit on a throne.

"It will be a singular honor for him," Henna was saying. "As you know, I have always observed the ancient ways. Why, before we began to number our dynasties, the King was *always* sent to his god if the land was threatened with drought. His hair was as red as the desert in the glare of noon. Like Pepy's." (Like *yours*, he thought. What there is of it.) "Ra-red it was called, and the god particularly welcomed such avatars.

Only of late has the color been thought unfortunate."

"To ride with Ra in his golden chariot across the heavens," said Ayub with the enthusiasm of high ambitions and low principles. "To see the Nile spread out like a sleepy snake. What more could a little boy ask?" Ayub was not a typical priest. He was neither ascetic nor plump. Tall, lithe, leonine, handsomer than any other man in Egypt (Harkhuf of course was in Yam), he tossed his magnificent mane and looked like the kind of lion which you can admire from a distance but must approach on tiptoe and with a bow in hand. "One thing is sure. Grown, he will be a disaster to Egypt. Well-intentioned but nevertheless disastrous. From laws to religion to war. He worships Ra in public but prays secretly to Osiris, the peasant god. And young as he is, he already wants to import that strange animal the Bedouins ride—camel is it called?— into our army. It is time to act. Already he goes among the people disguised as Harpocrates. They are coming to love the shadow who brings them gifts in the night. They are coming to call him a god. When they learn that Harpocrates and Pepy are one and the same, why, then he will be a king in truth. You, my lotus, are destined to rule in Egypt. I believe that Ra himself has called the boy to his side."

"But will it be painful?" asked Henna, a wisp of doubt in her voice. She is not completely a Taueret, Pepy concluded. Give her another year with Ayub. "Joining the god, I mean? As you know, the spirit of every pharaoh must battle the serpent Apophis before he can join Ra. After all, Pepy is only twelve."

"But he can out-run a gazelle and out-wrestle an orangutan," laughed Ayub.

"And how shall we start him on his way?"

"There are three acceptable methods."

"I know, I know," she snapped. "How should I not,

being a princess? Fire, poison, knife. What I do not know is the least painful method. After all, he is my only brother. I am rather fond of him in his docile moods. I should like to ease his passage as much as possible."

"I suggest the bite of the fu."

"The horned viper! Is it not a slow and agonizing death?"

"It is also the death most dear to the gods. And much the easiest to disguise as an accident for those misguided souls who mistake a ritual for an assassination." His whisper became a plea. "Dearest Henna. You are like a mother to him. I shall have to console you for his loss." He moved to embrace her.

"You forget yourself. I am Pharaoh's daughter. I am Pharaoh's sister. You are only a priest."

He laughed and shook his mane, a tangle of blacknesses in the lesser black of night. The lion was rebuffed but not cowed. "No one, not even Ra, has ever decreed that a priest must remain continent. And princesses, whatever the law, generally love as they choose."

"I choose a loyal servant and not a lover."

"As servant and priest I will perform the rite in the accustomed manner. The bite. The mummification. The wooden coffin and the stone sarcophagus."

"I can only commend your piety. Still, to lose one's brother is not an easy thing. The gods are cruel in order to be kind." The voice of a martyr facing the crocodiles. "I shall weep, Ayub. I shall weep a Nile of tears." (Crocodile tears.)

Pepy returned to his couch and, fighting the fears of a child, attempted to be a man. He conjured an image of Harkhuf, his caravan leader. He saw the flaring nostrils, the full sensuous lips, the unruly, unscented hair, the broad shoulders and copper chest. He saw a warrior and friend.

I will sleep, he thought, and dream, and send my spirit to Yam, and whisper in Harkhuf's ear, "Friend who loved my father, protect his son! In time I will willingly join Ra in his solar chariot, as befits an aged Pharaoh. Allow me first a battle, an exploration, perhaps a wife, not Henna (and separate beds). Hasten to Chemmis and bring your men and your bows (and don't forget the dwarf)."

I will sleep and dream.

I will sleep and. . . .

Chapter IV

"A gross misunderstanding," said Harkhuf. Dedwen and his soldiers had returned to their tents. He would have liked to recall them (or would he?). "Your command of Egyptian is commendable but incomplete. To an Egyptian the word 'whore' implies a woman who sells her body to men for trinkets and gewgaws. A"—with an inadvertent gulp of pleasure—"free-living woman with cheap perfume and too much galena and a loud, hearty laugh."

"We are not far apart," said Immortelle, wide-eyed and earnest, a child who is trying to educate a backward parent (but the jasper nipples, how they twinkled, how *maturely* they twinkled . . .). "Though I see you lack an exact equivalent for what I am trying to say." Thoughtfully she caressed the gem with her versatile tongue. Harkhuf envisioned a young, sun-dappled gazelle lapping water from a crystalline stream. (Harkhuf envisioned an experienced courtesan proving the old Egyptian adage, inscribed on the wall of a certain pyramid, "The tongue is the way to a man's heart.")

The amber glow of rushlights gave to the cavern a dawn at once unnatural and alluring. Strange, the chairs and couches which imitated the roundnesses of a ripe and delectable woman. Strange, the mosaic river

—mollusc, crocodile, hippopotamus—with its manifold creatures caught in the unanimity of love. Ganesh, the elephant god, presided in splendid majesty over the place, and only Ganesh did not appear strange, for Egyptians were used to animal deities—cat, cobra, falcon. Once, however, the god seemed to wink, and *that* was surpassing strange.

"My people, the Houri or Golden Minikins," Immortelle resumed, "both men and women, expect compensation for their favors. Just as you say, we sell our bodies for gewgaws and trinkets and, depending upon our skill, treasures. How else shall we live? We are not farmers. We are not builders. Unlike our local kinsmen, we are not boatmen. You see, we are carefully taught since childhood in the temple of one whom you would probably call Hathor, the Lady of Love, and her beloved, the Lord of Love, Athtar. I don't think you have an equivalent of *him*."

"I should think not," exclaimed Harkhuf, shocked to his sandals at the need for a god of love. To a man, the arts of love came as naturally as learning to eat or walk. Only women must study and practice and prove.

"You see," she continued with the remorselessness of a wise and determined child, "we have three ranks among our women: Whore, Courtesan, and Concubine. We have no wives. We have no wish for wives."

"Not even to bear children?"

"I shall come to that. A wife is like an anchor. She holds you in place until you collect barnacles. And a husband is a mooring line which cannot be untied. Among our men there are Studs, Lovers, and Lords. As with the women they are trained from boyhood and each rank entails an exhaustive examination written on palm leaves with quill pens from the tails of peacocks, and years of intimate practical experience. I am still a Whore. But then, I am only seventeen. Shortly I hope to graduate."

"And after you become a Concubine?" His thoughts remained with "whore": the nacreous horns, the wide cerulean eyes, the silken hair, the feet with four fetching toes, the jasper nipples. . . .

"Well, Concubine is the highest. Then we can choose the man in whose harem we will live for the rest of our lives. Choose for ourselves. Isn't it a lovely thought? Tutu and I were planning and hoping, don't you see, to attain Concubine and Lord at the same time, and I would have joined his harem and become his first Concubine. And borne him a child or two to continue our ancient ways. (He wanted *three*.) We would both have been rich by then. You understand, of course, that on Sappharine there are several races. One like you, brown-skinned, five or six feet in height, though with tails which they tend and comb and display as the women of Crete, I am told, display their breasts. One a head or so taller and winged like the sacred Roc. And it is they we pleasure, and they who pay us with gold and gems. Both of these races have their own women, poor frumpish creatures, for wives, but it is us they desire, and it is we who please." A contemplative pause. "But they are there, and I am here, and grateful beyond mere words. You have already paid me, as it were, with your rescue and your courtesy. How shall I repay you?"

"Sing?" he asked as she undulated toward him, and a red nipple winked like the eye of the elephant god. (It must be my age, he thought. It must be my sight. Too many deserts ablaze with the light of Ra. *Everything* seems to wink.)

"I can read your heart, you know. It is one of my gifts. Oh, not about war and booty and explorations and such. But about love. You do not want a song.

And yet you hesitate to claim what is rightly yours."

"No, I mean yes, I mean I don't know. Well, just look at you, a mere child, and me a man of thirty." Girls had never appealed to him since he became a man. Women, yes—raunchy, free-living whores . . . whores?

"I have delighted a man of *forty*. And you—well, you would be a challenge, not a burden, in spite of your size. I can accommodate you, you know. And you are still comely. You make me think of a large bear, what with that tumult of fur atop your head."

"We call it hair."

"Hair then. And also, I think, a touch of wolf. As if you would like to eat me up. Still you hesitate. Are you afraid of indigestion?"

"I think that you are a child instead of a whore, and one who needs a spanking."

"Dearest Harkhuf, how many times must I tell you that I am not a child?" A curious redolence permeated the air. Oleander? Nard? No, it was more like the scent of a brothel, compounded equally of smoke and beer and sweat and tallow and myrrh. The cave, once alien, now seemed familiar; the rushlights guttered and dwindled; the silken mat assumed the look of a couch. He had the distinct sensation that he was in his favorite of all Egyptian establishments, a brothel in Memphis.

"Well, sing for me first and we shall see."

"Very well." And this is what she sang:

The Concubine stirs on her rubicund couch
(The Lover dwindles and fades like a dying fire):
Alone, alone,
Forsaken by sleep,
Companioned only by shadows and wind
And remnants of Dream like shards of sound.

Listen!
It is the tread of her warrior, come from the wars.
She flings the amorous coverlet from her breasts;
Stands, incarnadined in the light of a lamp
Curved like a lotus bud;
Roses and amber awaiting richer than Dream.
Ah, he is lordly from conquest.
Ah, he is weary from conquest.
Let him be conquered. . . .

"There now. In the shadow of Ganesh, the elephant god, we shall offer the gift of love. He is a friend to lovers. Is his trunk not a sort of phallus? Lie still, my Harkhuf, my warrior and lord, and Immortelle will conquer the conquerer. First the sandals."

"My feet are dirty."

"How not? They are the feet of a warrior. I shall bathe them."

She drew a kerchief, a translucency of unknown material, from the bodice of her gown—no, it *was* the bodice of her gown—and bathed it in a ewer of holy water. "Now you are walking on air." Then, with a simplicity which was as artless as it was affecting, she unloosened his sandals and bathed his feet.

"My feet are cold." In fact they were hot; they felt as if he had trodden, barefoot, the Red Desert and the Green Wilderness. In fact, the whole of him was hot, from his burning feet to the tumult of hair which Immortelle had mistaken for fur. The brothel scent had gone to his head like beer; the red nipples, by Ra's holy rod, confronted him *without a screen*, like tiny moons emerging from a cloud.

"Never mind. They shall soon be warm. There now. Let's see, where does it fasten, the cloth that frames your splendid loins?"

Such a taking phrase: "splendid loins"!

"Here," he said, helpful even if doubtful. How to explain his doubts? She was young but hardly a virgin; he was eager as well as experienced. By her own admission, she owed him a debt and he was usually an avid collector. Still, the hesitation. Why? The truth lay deeper than he cared to probe, the deepest fish in the deepest bend of the Nile. The truth was a question which he did not like: *who was the fisherman and who was the fish? And what was the nature of the fisherman's hook?*

"Ah, the jade pin. Sly little creature, she would keep you to herself. Nestle selfishly against your thigh. But she is not to have her way. Nimbly, nimbly, my fingers, rout our mutual foe. Patience, perseverance, conquest!"

"Are there additional verses to your song?"

"My lord no longer wishes a song, I think. He understands that I am not a child, but a woman of some experience and much gratitude. He might have killed me. Enslaved me. Instead, he has become—my lord."

"Immortelle," he murmured. "The Immortal One?"

"The lover dies. Love endures. Is it not so?"

"I have small knowledge of metaphysical things."

"My lord has never known an abiding love?"

"I was wed by my parents at the age of fourteen. Before that, there had been the occasional rustic, the serving maid, the great lady or two or three. . . ." He tried to envision the occasionals; he could only see the immediate.

"My lord has never been in love. Poor Harkhuf. Is that wretched wife awaiting you back in Egypt?"

"No, thank Hathor. She was eaten by crocodiles."

"Exactly what she deserved." Now she had moved the gifts from the mat in front of Ganesh, and the

mat had become a couch. Now she insinuated herself
into his no longer reluctant, indeed reliant, arms.

"Whore," he murmured, and seized upon her with
bruising strength. ("My lord is a lion in love," he had
often been told. Except by Ti.)

She returned his kiss with a tongue whose agility
approached sorcery. "I am the lyre. You are the lyrist.
Draw from me songs to conjure a dragon out of the
deeps or summon a roc from the sky."

"Am I playing you well?" he demanded.

"My lord leaves me speechless with his aptitude."

"INDEED." Suddenly and sharp as the snapping
string of a lyre, the voice was familiar, the voice was
impossible.

He searched the shadowy corners of the cave.

"I thought," he whispered, "I thought that I heard—
no, I couldn't have heard."

"I too, my lord. Surely someone spoke."

"INDEED."

Her presence was undeniable. In the shadows, yes;
herself a shadow, yes. But irrevocably, nakedly Ti, the
Princess of Babylon. With her stood a young man of
diminutive stature and no discernible clothing except
his horns; a Hourus, no doubt. Both of them scruti-
nized the room as if they had came to reclaim a lost
possession.

"Tutu!" said Immortelle.

"Ti," said Harkhuf.

"A jinn," she cried.

"A ka," he cried.

The ka or soul was supposed to ascend to Ra in his
solar chariot or linger on earth in its favorite haunts.
If it chose to linger, if Ra or Osiris commanded the
choice, why then, let it wear invisibility for a robe.
Unobtrusiveness for a cloak. Receive a gift of food
from time to time; guard a tomb against thieves or

crocodiles; but *never* disturb the visible and the living. A jinn, he assumed, was a Sappharine ka.

Harkhuf could see the flicker of rushlights through his wife; she was less than solid but more than invisible and decidedly obtrusive. How had the arrogant lips retained their smile? Ra, it was clear, Osiris perhaps, had rejected her from the Celestial Paradise (or had she rejected them?).

"My poor clumsy Harkhuf. You always made love with the grace of a rutting ram. I see you have finally resorted to a young and inexperienced virgin." Then to Immortelle: "There, there, my dear. Some men are tender instead of rapacious. Some are gazelles instead of rams. Or so I am told."

The change in Immortelle was that of a gentle dolphin espying a predatory shark; the dolphin no longer chuckles and frolics; she *rams;* and Isis helps the shark.

Turning her adoration from Tutu, who remained in his place, she fixed her fury on Ti.

"Virgin. *Virgin!* I have never been so insulted." The four tiny fingers clenched into a fist. Physical blows seemed imminent. "Not since I was eleven. I have met your kind before, and let me tell you, Old Woman, if you were more than a garrulous mist, and my dear Tutu were still his substantial self, he would teach you what a dirty and disgusting word you have used. The only excuse for a woman to remain a virgin beyond the age of fifteen—eleven on Sappharine, a tropical island—is pitiable homeliness or unforgivable selfishness. Of which you think me guilty I do not know, but your insult is equally offensive in either case. If you had not already been devoured by crocodiles, I would conjure a great ravening bull to slither out of the Nile and drag you to his mate. And as for Harkhuf, my dear benefactor, you have insulted him too. Do you think I blame him for making love like a rutting ram? It is you who have left him in his pathetic ignorance. It is for me to teach him the arts of amorous dalliance."

"Ignorance?" roared Harkhuf, regaining his speech in the face of these unbelievable women, the golden fury and the speaking mist.

"Never mind, my dear. It is my concern, not yours. Lovemaking is both my pleasure and my profession. Now you must let me greet Tutu. How he escaped from my pendant I shall never know."

"*She* taught me how," said Tutu in a voice without rancor but with a hint of reproach. "A Babylonian conjuration." As golden as Immortelle, golden hair a rushlight about his head, he was a smooth young man who somehow did not appear soft; a young man with a face which might have looked feminine except for the resolution of the chin and the jaunty set of the horns, a young man made for love instead of war—soft couches, flickering candles, amorous intimacies—but made to *rule* in love, not to be ruled. "But she forgot to teach me how to walk. It was all I could do to climb out of the jewel. I was so cramped and bent, you see. Now I feel like a newborn cub. Surely my legs will collapse if I take a step. Immortelle, will you give me a hand?"

She hurried to his side and supported him as a swimmer supports a tilting papyrus bark. "It was the only way I had of keeping you with me—magicking you into the starry pendant, I mean. Otherwise, you would have wandered without a home and fallen prey to demons or loneliness or—"

"Followed you," he said. "I would have found a way."

"You will climb back into the stones?"

"No," he smiled, kissing her insubstantially on the

ear and somehow managing to leave a pink round imprint. "When has a Hourus ever shirked his duty?"

"Do you mean to say—?"

"Exactly. There is an enemy of love in our midst. I was only a Stud when I died, and Ganesh knows I have had no further experience, but the lady presents a challenge. There was nothing in our curriculum to prepare me for lovemaking with a mist, particularly when I share her insubstantiality. However, I am prepared to improvise. According to an old adage, 'Love is like an oyster. There are many ways of extricating the pearl.' Now if you will just guide my steps—"

"I *won't*," snapped Immortelle.

"Dearest one, can you doubt my heart?"

"N no," she confessed.

"From the time we were children, it was only you."

"True."

"Remember then the first lesson of our people: jealousy is the one forbidden emotion—until we attain the height. Now let my spirit be about its business."

"That pretty boy with horns is going to try to make love to *me*, a Babylonian princess?" cried Ti.

"Dearest lady," said Tutu. "There are few enough pleasures left to you now. Do not stand upon ceremony with one who wishes you well. Nobility in love consists of skill, not birth. If you must consider lineage, I too am descended from a king, and," he added, "of course a gazelle, though one with excellent blood." Then, dismissing Ti's objection with an ingratiating smile, he asked, "What did you like the best in the world of the living?"

Still smiling her aloof and superior smile but, so it seemed to Harkhuf, with a tiny lessening in resolution, and with a surreptitious look at Tutu, the kind of look in which a woman can evaluate a room or a person with one instantaneous sweep of her eyes, Ti said thoughtfully, "Aggravating Harkhuf."

"Did you," ventured Harkhuf, "did you by any chance abide in a certain Green Lotus and lure me into your petals?"

"Lure you, Harkhuf? You flatter yourself. I have already told you, I lived in your ring."

"I don't believe you," he said. "I—"

"Recriminations are for the dead," said Tutu. "Ti, my sweet, why did you wish to aggravate your husband?"

"Because I was married to him against my will, me, a princess, to a mere Egyptian nobody whose father had tilled the soil until he caught the eye of Pharaoh."

"Truly?" The word was undemanding; the tone demanded.

"Perhaps," she confessed, "perhaps I could have forgiven his birth if he had only shown a little respect. If he had remembered his place."

"Truly?"

"Oh, what is the use of pretending? I could have forgiven him his dirty fingernails, his unruly hair, his absolute abhorrence of a comb or a wig. I could have forgiven him everything, except that he hurt me and called it love. There was no courtship, you see. There was an arranged marriage between a big bully of a boy whose rustic parents had come into gold and a delicate and fastidious virgin whose aristocratic parents had lost their gold. Then, *pounce*, and I was supposed to pretend rapture and share him with great ladies or serving maids, whichever caught his eye, or let him go on the town like a randy goat and return to my arms with the stench of a whore's perfume."

"And what is wrong with a whore's perfume?" cried Immortelle. "I myself exhale a delicate musk.

Except of course at the moment. Harkhuf prefers, if I read his heart aright, a stronger scent he remembers from a place called a—a House for Cats. It does not please me, I grant, but who, Old Woman, am I expected to please, myself or my lover?"

"Whores are much more interesting than fine ladies. I have always wanted one for a friend."

By Ra's detachable beard, another voice in the room! The speaker, however, was truly invisible.

"Harkhuf, it is I, Pepy, and I have come to ask your help, only it is you who seem to need the help."

Silence fell upon the room like a great, entangling net. Another ka. This time Harkhuf's pharaoh, this time his friend. He felt an impotent rage. He wanted to bend a bow or cut a throat. Finally, a minnow of sound escaped from his lips:

"But I can't see you, Pepy. Are you also a ka?"

"Not yet. I came on the wings of sleep. My body is still on its couch in the palace of Chemmis."

"Then how can I help you, my son?"

"I am going to be murdered by Henna and Ayub and given a royal funeral to fool the people. They will put my heart in a jar and stuff the rest of me with spices and resins and then I shall be a mummy. I overheard them beside the lotus pool."

"But why, little friend?" cried Harkhuf. "Your sister is a bitch, I agree, and a hag to boot, but a murderess too?"

"Because of the phoenix. He came one hundred and ninety-nine years too soon and he didn't build a nest."

"Phoenixes be damned! Henna wants the throne."

"Ayub wants the throne. Henna had a dream."

"She dreams as she chooses."

"But she has never been wrong."

"Well, we shall see." He tried to encircle the invisibility with paternal arms but closed upon empty air. Then, without preamble, he bellowed like Aphis, the sacred bull, when he craves a cow:

"Dedwen, gather the men! We're returning to Egypt. Our pharaoh has need of us!"

"But the dancing dwarf—" (From the tents above the cave.)

"I have found one. Quickly now. Lower the tents. Load the asses. There is no time to be lost."

The two women and the young man looked at Harkhuf with a single expression: awe. A novice in love, according to Immortelle and Ti, but a leader without a peer, he was going to save his friend, Immortelle was coming with him to dance and sing. Tutu and Ti—well, let them do whatever a ka and a jinn were supposed to do at such a time, go or stay, dissolve or disperse.

Immortelle's pendant sparkled with resurrected fires and, Osiris be damned, he felt a warmth in the finger beneath his own amethyst ring! No matter. First he must get to Egypt and save his friend. Then he would worry about the perplexities thrust upon him by the ineptitude of crocodiles and the ardors of a young girl with horns and the unsuitability of releasing a naked young man from a pendant of starry stones.

First let him save his friend.

"There won't be time if we march," said Immortelle.

"Time? Once we reach the Nile above the first cataract—"

"But there are jungles and deserts to cross. Your little friend will die before you reach him."

"Do you know a quicker way?"

She uttered a piping noise like the cry of a bird.

Chapter V

He felt the reassuring warmth of Harkhuf, his eminence, his almost embrace; surely he heard his promise of help; met the jinn and the ka, the smooth young man from Sappharine and the prideful princess from Babylon. And the lady, Immortelle, his dancing dwarf.

He blinked his eyes and cleared the lingering sleep-mists from his brain. It was not a time to dream. Tike was born to dream; Pharaoh was born to do. He had called to Harkhuf for help. But more must be done.

Now, he felt a prisoner in his own bed, the raised pillow hard against his cheek, like a stone, like a fist. No one spoke in the courtyard under the moon. In the high, small windows which opened onto the court, intimations of morning stung his eyes. Dream had yielded to dawn and left him alone and afraid in his own friendless room, and he burrowed under the covers, a meadow mouse in a nest. *How can he reach me in time? The jungles, the deserts, the waters which lie between us—at best it will take him months.*

But tears, like hiding in dreams, were for little boys. He sprang from his bed and, barefoot, entered the garden, investigative, searching for traces of *them.* Here a broken lotus, there a sandal print in the dew-clean grass. Everywhere the faint, lingering scent of palm oil and priestly myrrh. Yes, they had truly met and plotted the means of his death (fire, knife, poison). Who except Harkhuf could help him in such a plight? To whom could he say, "My sister, the royal princess, and Ayub, the priest of Ra, are conspiring against my life?" He fancied an answer such as his elders would give him, priest, warrior, whomever he told, in the way of adults with children:

"Why, my child, do you think such a terrible thing?"

"Because I heard them plotting in the garden, beside the lotus pool."

"Heard or dreamed?"

"Heard."

"Again I ask why."

"Because they wish to be rid of me. Henna will be a queen and restore the ancient ways. And Ayub, I think, will murder *her*."

"And to be a queen she would kill her own blood kin?"

"Because of the phoenix, the drought, the famine, they said. In the old time, they said, the pharaohs were sometimes murdered to—to fertilize the fields."

"Sacrificed, not murdered. To sanctify, not fertilize. Only a bit of blood, perhaps an organ or two, was sprinkled among the crops. The rest was buried with proper rites. All was not bad in that time, in spite of your father's wrath."

To whom could he say such things? Who to believe him, believing, take his side? The army? Protected by sea and deserts, Egypt did not maintain an army in time of peace; every lord commanded his own guard, who promised allegiance to Pharaoh (but it was

Henna who gave them estates and gold). The palace
guard? Perhaps they preferred him to Henna, but fear
commands power. The lesser priests? Like Ayub, they
served the eternal Ra and his divine family, and what
fitter sacrifice than the son of the God? In earlier
dynasties, aging pharaohs had willingly gone to Ra
before their time to meet the will of the priests.

He, Pepy, was neither aged nor willing.

Pepy returned to his room and, rigid in one of those
stiff-backed chairs so different from the assorted
roundnesses in his dream, waited for Jacinth to super-
vise his toilet.

"My lord looks weary. Did he not sleep well?"
Jacinth bathed his brow from a brass ewer and
smoothed the recalcitrant hair into a semblance of
order.

"Jacinth, I am going to skip my bath this morning."

"*Truly?*" thundered the slave. Pepy might have said,
"I am going to war with the Bedouins or desecrate
the temple to Wazt, the cobra goddess."

"I dreamed too much, I think."

Mollified, Jacinth suggested a soothing posset, "before my Master goes to the temple to greet the
awakening of his Divine Father."

Merciful Num, it was one of his days to accompany the image of Ra on its circuit of the town! It
was the festival day of Hathor, the Queen of Love.

"No. Bring me the Cup of Anubis."

"My Lord, the cup of prophecy?"

"At once, Jacinth."

"My lord wishes to—perhaps—anticipate and avoid
whereof I warned him?"

"You are a good friend to me, Jacinth. Would you
like to return to Nubia? After—after—I no longer
need you?"

"To one accustomed to red deserts, palm trees are

a desecration. I left a mother, a sister, cousins beyond
number, but all of them dear to me." (I would have
died, thought Pepy, before I became a slave.) "Yes,
one day I would like to return. But only when
Pharaoh no longer has need of his servant. I will fetch
the cup from the palace storerooms."

*Stairs beyond number, corridors serpentining like
dormant snakes, wine stored in pigskins, gold in shiny
ingots, coconuts ripe with meat and sweet with milk
and—will he never return?*

He returned before Pepy had finished envisioning
the coconuts.

"Please, Jacinth, stay with me."

"It is not meet. The cup is for kings, not slaves. My
lord will have magic for his companion."

Alone, he fingered the sacrosanct vessel of prophecy.
Black bronze, hammered by priests in a temple to
Ptah, the smithy god, the cup was dinted and scarred,
and cold from its earthen nest, and yet it warmed
Pepy's hands, and not with reflected warmth, and its
bak oil swirled to image Anubis, the jackal god, sender
of dreams, weaver of spells; together with Thoth, his
brother, magician god. Fur on his human body; head
of a jackal instead of a man: a scavenger, true, but
vultures and jackals and other scavenging beasts were
fed and honored where rotting corpses harbored the
demons of plague, those small, malevolent beings which
even Pepy I and all of his gathered legions had failed
to exorcise.

"Anubis," prayed Pepy. "You have befriended
pharaohs before me, told them the future. Then, at
the last, guided their souls to Ra. Do I need such a
guide?"

For answer, the god emerged from the cup; small-

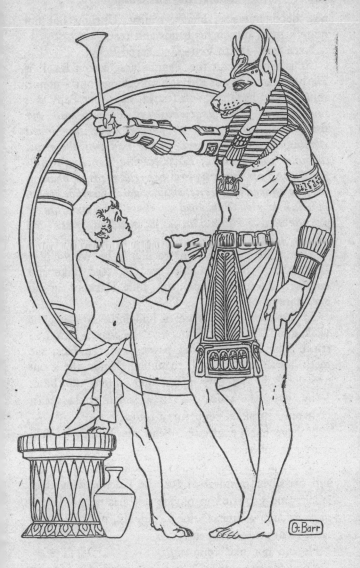

ness becoming size; image, reality. Upright but not
quite a man; fur on his hands and feet.

"Are you—? Are you—?" faltered Pepy.

"It is time to visit the Temple and waken Ra. It is
Hathor's day." It was Pharaoh's morning chore—honor,
some would have said—on festival days, but Pepy was
not deceived. *They have chosen to act with haste, my
sister and Ayub. It is they who have summoned
Anubis, Ra's own servant. In the midst of the ritual
to honor the Queen of Love, singing, dancing, drink-
ing black beer from hollow papyrus reeds, a pharaoh
may be effaced into a rite, a "surrogate" sacrifice which
in truth is real. Explained to those who question—if
anyone sees and questions—as an accident or the will
of the gods.*

Young, he did not want to die. Who would play
Harpocrates to his troubled people, feed Tike and
comfort the uncompanioned? Join Harkhuf in his
explorations of Yam?

At least the god wore a loincloth. At least he
walked on two legs. Otherwise, he was a jackal in
truth. The feet resembled paws. And the face, the
teeth like a row of small twinkling shields, the snout
prognathous, the ears upstanding above the head.
Why, even the voice . . . if a jackal could speak,
he would speak in such furry tones.

"I have not yet dressed. Send me Jacinth to help
with my toilet."

"Pharaoh has only to don his wig and his crown,
and his silver pectoral of Ra, the Falcon, winged in
jadeite and crowned in olivine. He has no need of a
slave at such a time. Quickly, quickly, my son. Your
father will grow impatient."

He did not like commands.

"You forget yourself," he said, reviving his courage

even as he reminded Anubis that Pharaoh, being the son of Ra, was also a god.

"Pharaoh is right." Doglike, he raised his upper lip to show his teeth. "I am only a messenger."

"Very well, then." It was useless to sulk in his room. Better immediate confrontation with his enemies; better a temple, a thoroughfare, a sacred grove, than a room in a palace shared with a jackal god. He donned the ceremonial wig and the Red Crown of the North. He clutched his uraeus staff, his possible club, and followed Anubis, the guide of the dead.

Frescoed corridor opened into court; court into hall; hall into the all-seeing eye of morning, and the many eyes of his people. Ah, the road to the temple might have been laid for a warrior's triumphal procession! Banners and obelisks and carpets as red as his crown. And people, people, people.

"Pharaoh," they shouted. "Save us from drought, save us from famine!" Did they guess the price of salvation?

Cripples on canes of bent cedar wood; whores whose shimmering ankle-long robes presented rather than concealed their breasts. ("Grow up, Pepy," they seemed to say. "We have surprises in store.") Ladies in carrying chairs like portable rooms. Tike too, waving a friendly hand, no more awed by Pharaoh than by Harpocrates.

They are my warriors, thought Pepy, they are my living walls. As long as I stay in the public eye, I am safe from Henna and Ayub. In the light of the sun, ritual murder seemed unthinkable. How could the bright god of day command a premature night for his chosen son?

Now, the ram-headed sphinxes; now, the pylon gate, twin towers linked by a linteled door; now, the temple to Ra, entered from the west where the chariot sun declined into the night, opening onto the east, where the sun began his climb. Four banners fluttered from four flagpoles emblazoned with signs of Ra: hawk; papyrus scepter; *tat* or four-barred symbol of immortality; uraeus serpent. The outer courtyard resounded with worshippers and reeked with offerings—plaited baskets heaped with triangular *shat*-cakes, trays of melons and large, rank-smelling onions prized by the multitudes, bags of geese and pigeons cleanly plucked for the fire. A market in miniature, even to the flies.

Then the hypo-style hall, a forest of thick, painted columns crowned with lotus buds, dim in the light of clerestory windows. Then, a lesser courtyard, a dwindling hall. . . . The *naos* or inner chamber, the room of the god.

A dreamer in stone and gems, the god slept in his nestlike niche; stood, to be sure, but the side-staring eyes seemed lost in dream. His head was that of a falcon, solar disk like a crest; beak like a curving blade to battle Apophis, the winged serpent, or Taueret, Queen of the South; human body encased in a gold-leaf robe like a mummy's shroud. So ancient and awesome a being could not be portrayed as a man; rather, a man with the head of that fierce bird which followed the flight of the phoenix into the sky and attained a view of the sun denied to other birds.

"But the *naos* is empty," said Pepy. Where were the priests to rouse the image of Ra with hymns of thanksgiving and crown his head with a hood and deck him with flaxen robes and carry him into the courtyard before his people?

"I am the God's emissary," said Anubis. "Are you afraid of me?"

"No. You aren't an executioner, you're only a guide."

"Still, I can read the fear in your eyes."

A shadow from then had darkened the sun of now. The old magic was not, after all, eternally locked in the South; Henna and Ayub had opened a gate. Nightmare had fled with Dream; Nightmare returned at the call of a priest and a princess, the first ambitious, the second reverent and cruel.

Pepy was fearful, yes. He felt as if furry caterpillars were crawling down his throat. Still, there was more than fear; there was curiosity warring with dread; there was exaltation. He did not want to die, he wanted fiercely to live, but he felt in the deepest catacomb of his heart that Dream and Nightmare were as different as Egyptians and Nubians, but as inseparable as lovers. Confront and conquer the Nightmare if you can, but never shut it away in a book of incantations, a box of incense and magic sticks, a land to the South. It will find a way to escape. Or else it will clutch and cling to the Dream and you will be safe and sane and comfortable but somehow— less. For once his father had not been entirely wise; his sister was heartlessly wise.

He did not think these things; he did not have time to think. He felt them and shuddered but did not flinch from his guide.

"Take me to Ayub and Henna." For they had opened the book, the box, the door to the South.

The grove was dedicated to Hathor as Lady of Love, not Marriage; widely spaced, the palms; softness of grass and clover between them; summer houses of bent papyrus stalks to invite the rugged boatman or the fastidious priestess; farmer and whore; men with their concubines, wives with their lovers. Here, in the understanding smile of the Lady, they took their delight while lyrists coaxed their lyres to stir the unyielding heart, the unresponsive limb. To Pepy, love was as enigmatic as a sphinx. Still, he could ponder its secret.

The Nile engirdled the island like a friendly snake. An intricacy of waters spiderwebbed from the life-sustaining river; canals dug by men, natural streams ablaze with pleasure boats. Remote (though remote was near on this little island), the sounds of the city were sweetened to music by wind in the palms. The cry of a vendor became a harvest song; the wheels of an oxcart thundered like drumbeats along an undulant road.

Pepy looked at his people and smiled with the pride of a pharaoh. He laughed when he saw the animals, dogs by the legion, monkeys a ceaseless chattering in the trees, and shameless baboons who romped and snorted and made a laughter of red-bottomed ugliness.

I have surely been drugged, thought Pepy. I have tasted no bread and drunk no wine, but something . . . the God . . . Anubis . . . the lure of this place . . . has woven a mist before my eyes and bewitched my ears until I can only hear a single unending song of zither and lyre, but where is the trumpet blast of battle and death?

I have surely been drugged to prepare me for the snake.

"Henna," he called, his voice peremptory in the dulcet air; strong for a boy. "Is it you who have planned this festival?"

"Pepy, Pepy," she smiled, her copper hair like a helmet bent in the sun, hard, blindingly bright. Her smile seemed hammered in bronze. "It is Hathor's holiday. The day when the Goddess, disguised as a giant cow, created the world, the Nile, the red desert and the black vineyard, the islands of the Great Green

Sea; and our own ancestors. Celebrate, little brother! Sing, dance, whatever you will!"

A shaking of sistrums urged him to take her advice. Hathor's priestesses, robed in white but smiling scarlet smiles, shook the cow-headed instruments in their brown, small hands. A little girl, urged by her mother, approached him on tentative steps and clutched a garland of bindweed and daisies.

"Here," she said, thrusting it toward him like a funeral wreath. He accepted the flowers without touching the hand, for she would have flinched from the touch of a god, and he hung them around his neck and smiled and stripped a bracelet of jadeite from his arm and flung it after her as she ran to rejoin her mother.

Do they know, he wondered, except for Henna and Ayub? My people, the priestesses, the whores, even the little girls? Have they come to witness the ritual sacrifice and send me to the God?

Anubis followed him like a shadow, smiling a doglike smile of parted lips and glistening teeth, padding softly upon the grass and clover. *How can they fail to recognize the god? Ah, but magic has fled to the South. My people believe in Ra, Hathor, Anubis, but who among them has seen a god in the flesh?*

Tike handed him a basket of berries and buttercups. Hathor's Delight, the berries were called. Large, ripe, succulent.

"I picked them myself." His face said "festival." His face said "food."

Gratefully, Pepy accepted the basket from his friend. He started to part the flowers and lift a handful of berries to his lips. He had neither eaten nor drunk since his awakening. Yet he had come to a festival to eat and drink with his people. Berries picked by Tike would seem a feast.

"And someone added the flowers. I didn't see who. I left the basket to pick some berries and then it was full of flowers. I 'ope you like them too."

The petals trembled as if in a breath of wind. The berries too—did they roll and settle because of their roundnesses?

"Pharaoh!" cried Tike. "You've washed your 'air and put on a royal crown. But you're really—"

Pepy lifted a cautioning finger to his lips.

"Of course," whispered Tike, " 'e's your *secret* self. I 'ave one too." He smiled with complicity and waited for Pepy (Pharaoh-Harpocrates) to enjoy the gift.

Two diminutive horns emerged from the flowers. Shy little horns, horns like feelers afraid of the light. A snail, a—

Pepy flung the basket onto the ground. Cries of disappointment shivered among the crowd. Pharaoh had dared to disdain a gift! Pharaoh had shamed a little fisherboy!

" 'Arpocrates!" wailed Tike, forgetting their secret.

Some of the berries, some of the petals, scattered around his feet. But the basket did not overturn nor dislodge nor even disclose the creature with horns.

"Pick it up," said Ayub. "Pharaoh *never* disdains a gift from his people."

"Pick it up, little brother," said Henna. "You must not disappoint a child."

Pepy retrieved the basket and saw why the berries had moved and saw too the horns attached to the head, and the head, startled, waving from side to side, attached to the tail of a snake. Not the cobra. Not the lethal hooded snake incarnated as the goddess Wazt. A young viper with horns. A *fu*.

Pepy's hands seemed frozen onto the basket. The head seemed molded from gold, the body from umber and onyx. Except that they moved. No one could see them except Pepy. Alone in a multitude, he met the hypnotic eyes, the eyes of death, and the smell of death was the sweetness of berries, but also the rankness of damp fur from a tomb, for Anubis, smiling, stood at his side.

"Come, Pepy." His voice was that of a father and friend; furry, though; animal.

"No!"

It was then that he heard the rush of wings, and a shadow replaced the sun, and he thought, "The phoenix has come again to witness the sacrifice."

Shadows, not shadow.

Birds, not phoenixes.

Harkhuf.

PART

II

Chapter VI

"Her name is Roseate."

"Oh? A female."

"Of course. The males are much too lazy to carry riders."

He had never expected to fly to Paradise on the back of a roc; he must climb, so he thought, the Celestial Ladder, rung over slippery rung, battling demons with every step, Apophis, the winged serpent, Aha with his tongue of fire. But now—

Wonders to see above him! See and touch and taste! The clouds were a wonder brighter than phoenix feathers. Clouds were rare over Egypt, numberless over Yam, and he seemed to descry celestial pyramids, pylons, thoroughfares, only to have them shift and dissolve and reform, as if they were made of sand and a heavenly wind had leveled or banked or reshaped them before his eyes.

And the colors. . . . How they twinkled and flourished, dimmed and flared, sun on the clouds, but more than gold: agate and hematite, jasper and peridot, but softer than gems; colors out of the Celestial Paradise. He reached to grasp and fondle these shapes of Dream, the Dream he had followed for much of his life, but his hands closed on empty air and he strained to borrow, if only for now; strained to remember, for the

77

time when the clouds were lost and sky reverted to earth. Image yielded to image; feathers, sand, gems. . . . Consistency was inconsistent with Dream.

He heard a music compounded of wind and wing-beat and—was it the song of the clouds, the shifting mists emitting a taunt and a tune?

Come, come, come, Harkhuf the proud,
Capturer, conquerer, capture us if you can,
(Harkhuf, the heavenly man).
Capture the lapis lazuli-turning-cloud,
The beryl which dies into jade which leaps into gold,
    Harkhuf, the bold. . . .

He tasted an exquisite moisture—cloud-wine?—and wondered if any vintage on earth could be half so sweet, or rush to his blood and warm him and cool him and make him drunk with color and sound and taste.

Thus do the gods enjoy celestial banquets.

He yearned to his mount as a Bedouin yearns to his camel. He felt the gigantic heart in this creature between his legs, this outsized bennu, this airborne and agile ostrich, this nonpareil. He was not being carried to Egypt, he was being delighted to Egypt as if by a playful dolphin, which naturally hearkened to man and loved to disport with him and show him its secret ways! The sloping body, the sudden lift, the leap into the sky, into the clouds, beyond the clouds, until—

He spun in the air like a minnow caught by a maelstrom. He fell, spiraled, plummeted.

"The roc has dropped me," he yelled. No, he clung to the crest, as a swimmer clings to a hippocampus' mane.

"Whoa," he shouted, accustomed to oxen and asses.

"Kneel," he shouted, thinking of Bedouin camels.

"*Don't let him know you're frightened.*" Immortelle. Her voice was a whisper above the wind. Whisper or thought?

Afraid! He, Harkhuf, afraid of a paltry bird?

Still, there were times to follow advice, even that of a girl.

"Hold on there now, fellow," he said, firm but affectionate. "Immortelle has given you a job and it's to get me to Egypt. *Whole.*"

For answer, a spin, a dip, a climb, a sudden dart to the left, a tilt to the right.

"If you unseat me, I'll take your crest and half of your feathers! You'll look like an overstuffed goose ready for the spit!"

For answer, a loop like a somersault in a Nile cataract.

Harkhuf, the fearless, tasted the viper venom of fear.

Then, another voice, slightly acidulous (typically acidulous). "If you had a little respect for our sex—"
Ti.

"Now, now, my dear," he said coaxingly to Roseate, the female. (A male would not have deceived him; lulled him into a foolish sense of fun.) "Fly me gently and I will spruce your feathers with an ivory comb."

He poised for another spin.

"And string your tail with costly ribbons." One thing he knew: how to sweet-talk a woman. "When you get me safely to Egypt." It was hard to speak, what with the speed and the jolts. It was well to speak, if he wished to save his life.

He had, it seemed, survived the cataract; now, he might have been riding a tranquil river in a bark of papyrus. You could measure the flap of the wingbeats —lift and lower, lift and lower—precisely as oars in the hands of Pharaoh's own boatmen.

"Are you all right?" Immortelle. (Thought or words?)

"I have broken no bones, I think. As for torn ligaments, I suppose they will mend."

"I can't understand why Roseate lost her manners. Perhaps because you are new to her, and heavier than Tutu, and, forgive me, less gentle, and—"

"More manly."

"Well, you seem to have won her affection at last. I never saw such bliss in her eyes."

He stroked the fern-large feathers and tried to ignore the smell. (*The animal needs a bath. Musty. Smells of the nest. Broken eggs. Greedy fledglings as big as full-grown vultures.*)

"Harkhuf, my dearest," said Immortelle.

Her "dearests" were starting to cloy. Still, it was wise to appease her in the air. A roc, a Minikin, an immaterial ka: women, all of them, they had him in their power. At such a time, honesty was a broken sword, flattery a shield and a spear.

"Is my lord comfortable?"

"I have already said—yes, I am fine." Useless to number the aching ligaments.

"Stop clinging, my dear. *Abide.*"

"Very well," he sighed, abiding. Then, forgetting his aches, "Do you think we will reach him in time? Pepy, I mean."

"Trust me. Trust Roseate." (Ha! As soon trust a spotted sphinx.) "Such a dear child, your Pepy. How wicked of Henna to want to murder him before he has sampled the fruits of love! Or has he? On Sappharine, boys of twelve have already tasted the rarest pomegranates. The Minikin boys, I mean."

"Indeed?" muttered Harkhuf. "I would have put the age at eight. For the girls, anyway. Bananas, of course, not pomegranates."

"And the local folk are learning from us," she said, ignoring his petulance. "After all, we are expert guides. I myself have taught a boy of nine."

"Oh? A trifle young, I would say." Harkhuf had tasted his first pomegranate at the age of eleven, a serving girl. The experience had been more instructive than pleasurable; she had wept and pouted; he had climbed a tree to hide from her furious father.

"But Pepy is a trifle old. It might be that I myself could introduce him to the—"

"Pepy is *Pharaoh*," snapped Harkhuf. "He has no time for amorous dalliance."

"He did seem a bit over-serious. A pity. Even a pharaoh should take his moments of ease."

"He hunts with me in the Delta. He has already killed six crocodiles and three hippopotami, to say nothing of saving a nest of baby basilisks from a vengeful cobra."

"What does he do at night?"

"Sleeps, what else? Now to matters at hand. How will we get to Chemmis in time to help?"

"You cannot guess the speed of these birds. No jungles to tramp. No deserts to trudge. Only the airwaves to ride. I have simply said, 'Follow the Nile,' and the Nile, you have told me, leads to Chemmis."

"In truth, though, the river divides and the Delta is somewhat confusing. At the proper time, I will act as guide. Meanwhile, is Tutu with you?"

"Oh yes. I won't drop him. He's safely ensconced in my pendant. In fact I can feel his heartbeat against my breast. And Ti?"

"Her ring is a bit loose on my finger. I do hope it won't be lost in flight."

"Have no fear. Ti would change her lodging before she fell. That is to say if kas are like jinns. Quick,

don't you know. Adaptable. She might even embody
herself in your loincloth."

Did he hear a strident snort?

For three days they followed the Nile. Immortelle
had provided food, bananas and breadfruit, flagons of
palm wine, cheeses wrapped in enormous lotus pads.
Cooled by the breeze of their flight even in windless
regions, feasted on luscious fruits, they saw the
demonic jungle yield to the desert, the desert vacillate
between sandy wastes and wasted stone outcroppings,
they saw the camps of those Desert-Crawlers, the
Bedouins, black tents like spiders in the sun; but always the blue-black river, sometimes brightening into
green, sometimes blanching into white, forever under
them; cataract yielding to cataract; towns, fortresses,
Egypt.

Then, the North; the many-watered Delta; the
place of palaces and the place of fear. Afloat in its
malachite lake, the island of Chemmis looked as in-
nocuous as a jellyfish, concealing poison beneath its
many colors.

"Where shall we land?" called Immortelle. "I see a
town and also a palace. Walled. Columned. Grilles instead of windows. Everything built of sun-dried bricks
compounded with strips of linen. There are prettier
palaces on Sappharine, but at least the roof is flat. It
might make a landing place."

"A bit lower." His keen eyes could hardly distinguish the town, much less the palace. Cautiously, jerk-
ing their heads from side to side, the rocs descended
the cloudless sky. Harkhuf felt the quickening heart-
beats of Roseate, the curiosity in her female breast.
About to alight on a god-sired pharaoh's roof! Was
she anticipating the honor to her flock (or the ribbons
for her tail)?

Harkhuf peeled his explorer-trained eyes.

"I see a crowd. A festival, I think. Pharaoh always goes to a festival. It's part of his job."

"I see him quite clearly," announced Immortelle. "That staunch little fellow with red hair. Someone is giving him a basket of fruit. A fisherboy, I think. Now he is dropping the fruit. Merciful Ganesh, a horned viper is wriggling out of the basket!"

"You can see all that?"

"And an ugly woman in a red wig. Henna, no doubt. I believe I saw her smile!"

"Land the birds in the crowd!" cried Harkhuf. "The viper is meant for Pepy."

Even as Harkhuf leaped from his aerial steed, Pepy ran toward him, laughing, and it seemed to him that in all of his thirty years, in all of his adventures, amatory and exploratory, he had seen no sight to surpass the running, laughing boy.

"Oh, Harkhuf, Harkhuf, how I have missed you! And you have answered my dream and come to save me. And brought me the dancing dwarf."

It was not a pharaoh he held in his arms, it was his friend's little boy, *his* little boy, and he almost resented love's exacting bonds. Shackles of bronze could not have held him more surely than this brave, imperiled child. In the past, bondage had meant a horror to him; obligations and duty—these were for slaves and kings. He was born for freedom, meant to explore; stranger to cities, alien to houses, friend to a tent or a camp.

Still, the small but persistent arms—could he shake himself free of them? Was love not a freedom as well as a bondage, a soaring more surely than that of a risen roc?

"I am not a dwarf," said Immortelle with firmness but not asperity.

"A *dancing* dwarf, I said. I will give you bracelets of silver and anklets of gold. And you will dance for Harkhuf and me. Once I am rescued, that is to say."

"Don't misunderstand me. The payment sounds munificent. But you mistake my profession as well as my race. I dance and sing, to be sure, and what have you—"

"What do you have?"

"Well, my breasts have been likened to the Apples of Love. Observe the red of the nipples."

"Allow me a closer look. Yes, quite red I would say. Edible, so to speak. Perhaps you could teach my sister—"

"My lord Harkhuf," said a voice which, attempting honey, achieved salt. "You have chosen a strange and dramatic fashion to invade the festival of our Lady Hathor."

"Drama seemed necessary," he said, deftly stomping his foot on the viper's head. The sly little snake had pretended sleep among the fallen flowers; now, he was peering at Pepy's foot, hopeful, no doubt, of a second chance.

"Do you deny us obeisance to the gods? It seems propitious these days, what with the Nile about to withhold his flood."

"You have been dreaming again, dear Henna. Perhaps if you shared your couch with a man, your dreams would be less—perverse."

"My lord Harkhuf, *I have said that*—"

"Spare me, Henna, your lurid fancies."

"My lady's fancies generally come to pass." It was Ayub, taller by half a head than Harkhuf, heavier, brawnier, a priest who looked like a warrior; a warrior's son who had deigned to become a priest in order to strengthen his power. His voice was bronze, his hand seemed fashioned to grip a spear instead of a staff. He was not a man to be cowed. "Her dreams have guided Egypt since the death of your friend, Pepy I."

"Egypt is not an army, she is a people. What do *they* think?" He pointed a meaningful finger at the crowd.

"What they are told."

"Do they? I wonder."

Ladies and whores, lords and river men, they had turned the meadow into a marketplace. Silent, yes— who would have dared to interrupt a discourse between a great explorer and a young pharaoh, lately arrived by roc, with a high priest and royal princess?— but straining to overhear the curious exchange, even while glancing from time to time at the birds.

"Do not underestimate me, Harkhuf," said Henna, wry but commanding. "Do not confuse the woman with her dreams. At me the people laugh. The women mock my wigs and what lies under them; the men deplore my want of a bosom. But when I tell them my dreams, they plan, journey, dig, build, sail, marry, and procreate. As you and Pepy should know, the gods use dreams to communicate with men. I am a princess. I am also a seeress. Nilus has sent me a dream of drought and famine. The people believe me. You too, I think. You have come from the South on the backs of fabulous birds. Something called you home. What, may I ask?"

"Pepy came to me in a dream."

"It is given to him to walk abroad in a dream. It is given to me, his sister, to read a dream."

"The Nile is angry," said Ayub. "You, the mighty explorer—can you appease the god? Prevail upon him to relent and release his nurturing waters?"

"Why, by the Blue Hippopotamus, is he angry?" asked Harkhuf. His mind did not run to theological matters. Gods should stay in the sky or under the earth and listen to prayers. They should only exact a punishment if you forgot to pray. Then, the propitious sacrifice, a lamb, a calf, whatever suited the god in question—a jackal sufficed for Ra but offended Anubis—should appease the divine wrath.

"My dream did not enlighten me," said Henna. "After all, I am not Pharaoh. All I know is the fact of Nilus' anger."

"Why, then," said Immortelle, glaring at Henna, "we shall have to learn for ourselves. In the land of Yam, there is an oracle, a river-cave, often visited by the local Minikins. When they wish to question the god, they swim to his cave, and Nilus speaks to them with his watery tongue. He is never wrong. We shall have to return to Yam and ask him for ourselves."

Harkhuf deliberated. He could not leave Pepy with Henna and Ayub. If not a snake, then a knife . . . if not a knife, then a fire. Could his roc support a second body in flight?

"Harkhuf," said Immortelle. "Pepy can ride with you. The roc will scarcely notice the extra weight."

"Of course," he said, and sensing that Ayub had hidden men in the crowd, he quickly hoisted his pharaoh onto his shoulders and clambered onto his bird.

"Ho there, Roseate," he commanded. "Back to Yam."

Roseate hugged the ground as if she had broken a wing. No, she drew her wings like a cloak around her body. Isis, he swore. She wants to relieve herself, but the crowd has filled her with shame. How typical of a woman. You start on a journey and where is your wife? Locked in the water closet.

"You have forgotten your promise," said Immortelle.

"Promise?"

"The ribbons for her tail. How typical of a man."

"Tike," suggested Pepy, apprising the situation. "Can you find her a ribbon? Something large and gaudy?"

As if by the subtle hand of Harpocrates, a voluminous lady dressed in the new Cretan style—filmy bodice and belled skirt—suddenly lost her film. Plump as a mother goddess, she smiled at the gaping crowd and shook her abundances. Tike, it seemed, had learned from his idol, Harpocrates. But who had taught him to drape the tail of a bird? Whoever, he draped with skill and without entangling the feathers or preventing flight.

"Stop that urchin," cried Henna. "He has disrobed a lady."

"We shall have to take him to Yam," said Pepy. "Otherwise, Henna will feed him to the crocodiles."

"Here, Tike," said Immortelle. "You can ride with me," and he clambered behind her onto the downy back.

"Do you like fish?" he asked.

"Fish but not meat. You see, my great-great-great-grandmother—give or take a few great's was a gazelle."

"Does the Nile flow all the way to Yam?"

"Oh yes. And through. And beyond."

"Once we get there, I'll whistle you the fattest carp in all the river."

Roseate, decked with a crimson bodice if not a ribbon, flapped her wings and rose above the crowd and poised in the air, like a coy dragonfly, to display her finery.

"Pharaoh," shouted Ayub above the noise of the wings.

"Pepy," shouted Henna. "Will you leave your people to starve?"

"Whatever the god decrees, I shall return. Pharaoh has given his word." Pharaoh in truth.

Anubis, gently smiling, observed the ascent of the birds and waved his hand.

Harkhuf mistook him for a priest. "Pepy, he is a friend?"

"Yes, I expect, in eighty years or so."

"I don't understand."

"Never mind. He does."

And so they flew to Yam.

Chapter VII

Aquamarine.

"It isn't a city, it's a fleet," said Pepy.

"It's an *armada*," said Tilto wrongly emphasizing the first syllable, since the Egyptians, at home on the Nile but terrified of the Great Green Sea, had never built an armada, and only the Cretans could boast such a formidable power.

Fleet or armada, it was built for peace. In a lake beside the Nile, fed by the river but hushed from its turbulence, the Brown Minikins had moored their floating city. Jetties of baobob timbers . . . houseboats, brighter than water-lilies . . . lianas serving to moor and bind . . . sails folded as neatly as petals for the night . . . oars like stems on the decks.

"You see," said Immortelle, "the boats are a stationary town, but in time of danger—an attack from the Black Dwarves, for example—the Minikins raise their sails, lower the oars, and off they speed into the Nile, and nobody, not even a crocodile, can overtake them. They used to moor in another lake, but that was before the Green Melancholy. The Lotus was always there, but not the sorrow. There was nothing to do but find another lake. There were actually suicides before the move! Even here they catch an

G.Barr

occasional sadness on the wind. But the boats are once again their homes. On Sappharine, of course, which is free of dangers, we live in cities with domes and walled gardens of mulberry trees and something for which you have no word—minarets."

The houseboats suggested the typical river craft of Egypt—perhaps Egyptian builders had learned from Minikins in a time before scribes had recorded history. The prow and stern were raised like the outer petals of a cupping flower. The sails, however, did not suggest Egypt. The Minikins called them "lateen"— billowy triangles instead of rectangles, affixed to a bending mast. In the middle of the deck, a circular cabin with walls of bundled papyrus reeds replaced the square Egyptian canopy. Even the jetties were curved instead of straight. Everywhere, curves, circles, and crescents supplanted straight lines and rectangles, grace was wedded to power, though the builders were sailors and warriors and, when necessary, manual workers, and their four-fingered hands were calloused from hammer and spike, their horns suggested weapons instead of adornments. It was even said of the women, who looked like Egyptian dolls, that they could de- liver a baby and rise from their couches to wield an oar or sling a boomerang. Even now, both men and women were scurrying over their decks, lighting lanterns, preparing supper on movable grills with the speed and agility of those to whom work is a privilege instead of a burden.

But back to the boats. . . . It was hard to leave Aquamarine, even in thought. Lanterns twinkled from every bow. By night, the city resembled a mating dance of fireflies; vessels shimmered; reflections trem- bled—surface city and sunken city—and curving jetties seemed to be paths laid down by the moon.

"But the city is *you*," said Pepy to Immortelle.

"Oh no, our cities on Sappharine are much different, as I have said."

"It's still you," he persisted. "Grace and strength."

"Grace I can claim. I was born with some, taught some. It goes with my profession. But hardly strength."

"Strength too," he said with gentle emphasis. "The best of Brown and Gold."

"Strength," she mused. "Do you really think—?"

"Oh, yes," said Pepy, imagining his palace on Chemmis with Harkhuf, Tike, and Immortelle. "You see, he doesn't suspect the extent of your power." It was hard to confess a weakness in his god; it was harder not to be Pharaoh and just.

"Pepy," she sighed. "Sometimes I think you are forty instead of twelve."

"Henna has aged me."

"I didn't mean you look old. I mean you sound old. Perspicacious, I would say."

"I don't know the word. Is it good?"

"Yes. Now you and Tike shall have your special boat."

Pepy had never slept in a boat. When he traveled, it was in a carrying chair which was more like a portable room. Ten carriers, it took, stalwart Nubians with broad backs and skins conditioned to sun and sand. Or he traveled by gilded barge, which was towed or rowed, depending upon the condition of the Nile, with the portable room on the deck instead of the backs of the men. When they moored for the night, the room was set on the shore to escape the sway of the river and pegged securely into the ground, the carriers stood guard, and Pepy slept in a small but comfortable bed complete with mosquito net to withstand those tiny black demons (Bedouin *kas*, said the priests) who swarmed through the cracks to wreak their vengeance on the builders of dams and cities.

Here, in the jungles of Yam, Pepy had been prepared to rusticate and fight mosquitoes and share discomfort with Harkhuf and his men. But the boat was a palace except in size.

Tike had only slept in a canvas tent, and then on his fortunate nights, when a kindly river man, or a lonely whore, offered a lodging in return for a song. Unfortunate nights, he slept in the open and risked not only mosquitoes but scorpions, spiders, and snakes.

"I'll 'ave to whistle a *river* of fish to make up for this," said Tike, looking about him at the palatial surroundings. "Our own bed with a tent—"

"Canopy."

"What's that ivory stick for under the bed?"

"It's a wand. You wave it in circles over the bed and bring yourself luck."

"We already 'ave our luck. And our own—what is that 'ippopotamus breathing out smoke? 'As he caught fire?"

"Tike, remember your 'h's.' He's a brazier. The nights get cold in the jungle. Or so Harkhuf says."

"And what by Anubis' tail is that?"

"A portable water closet."

"Oh," said Tike. "We could do without that, what with the lake and all. Never mind. Who am I to complain? A bed and a wand for luck and a smoking 'ippopotamus. Pharaohs sure 'ave it easy."

"Pharaohs also get murdered in their beds."

"Even with ivory wands?"

"Sometimes their enemies have stronger wands."

"And fisherboys who share the same beds?"

"They don't get murdered. They've nothing anybody wants."

"Nothing at all?" cried Tike, looking as if he had lost a fish from his line.

"Except their songs," Pepy hurried to add, seeing his friend's disappointment. "And one song is worth a dozen palaces. In fact, a palace may start with a song."

Tike appeared mollified. "Well then, I'm very tired, and I think I'll wave our wand and practice not rolling out of the bed. Possibly I shall sleep *under* the bed. That way, if the wand should fail and enemies should lurk about, I can 'appen upon them and save your life."

"First you must eat," said Pepy, taking charge in the fashion of pharaohs when Henna was not at hand. Really, Tike *did* need instruction as well as indulgence. "You're much too thin, Tike. A crocodile would need two of you to make a satisfactory meal. I think you should start with a stew of oryx and ibis, together with lentils and onions—"

"No onions, please."

"*Onions.* They'll thicken your blood and help you develop muscles in those skinny arms and throw off demons."

"Very well, 'arpocrates," said Tike, fingering his flute and, since he had been temporarily forbidden the bed, looking as if he would rather play or sing than eat.

In fact, he improvised a song:

> "An oryx and a pumpkin stew,"
> The Pharaoh Pepy said.
> "A lentil and an onion *too*
> Before you go to bed."

> "Perhaps a pumpkin and a steak"
> (The fisherboy) "but *not*,
> Together with a stomach ache,
> An onion in the pot."

> "A pumpkin and an oryx (hot)
> And *then* an onion too
> Or would you like a hippopot-
> Amus stirred in your stew?"

> "An onion, please, will do."

"Egyptian poems shouldn't rhyme. Eat!"

But the dinner was soon invaded by uninvited guests, and not Harkhuf, unfortunately, who was counseling with the Minikins. Immortelle was the first guest.

Calling the boys' names, she parted the whispery rushes of the door and stepped into the lamplit circle. Her gown was as blue and festive as a forget-me-not, her hair was as gold as a buttercup, but she looked as if she expected a thundershower. Though the lips were properly curved for a smile, a single tear descended her pink cheek like an indiscreet snail.

"Did my boys enjoy their dinner?"

"No meat," said Tike. "Pepy talked about oryxes and steaks, but all we got was vegetables."

"Oh?"

"*Onions.*"

"But the Minikins are vegetarians. As you know, we claim descent from a certain famous gazelle. If we didn't stick to vegetables, we might find ourselves eating a relative."

"But *onions?*"

"You ought to be in bed, both of you," she admonished, though not in the horrid way of sisters. "Three days in the air and you must be exhausted. Rocs are not smooth riding, on the whole."

"Yes," said Tike. "I was just saying to Pepy—"

"No," said Pepy. "First, Tike must finish his supper. He's much too thin. Besides, he's hidden an onion under his lentils. Then I would like to have you dance for us." She had not explained why she danced but did not call herself a dancer. Was she not the dwarf whom Harkhuf had found for his court? The object of his first expedition into Yam?

"Pepy, my dear, I think you misunderstood my profession. I am not a dancing dwarf. I am a Golden Minikin, more precisely a Houri."

"A whore!" he cried, smoothing the tumult of hair atop his head and wishing his loincloth were clasped with a blue steatite scarab instead of a rusting solar disk. "Why, that's better than a dancer. You can do more. I see them every day in Chemmis—they smell like overripe fruit, but there's always a twinkle in their eyes, and they don't seem to think me unlucky because of my red hair and freckles. You don't smell like fruit. You smell like grass and flowers. I've never had a whore for a friend, though."

"Yes, my dear, I am proud to say that I am both a Whore and your friend, and in my profession, the arts of the dance are subordinate to the Art of Pleasuring in general, and one pleasure in particular."

Pepy looked perplexed; he cast a surreptitious glance at Tike to see if the fisherboy, who lived in the streets, knew more of such particulars, but Tike divided his attention between Immortelle and his flute and it was hard to tell if he was admiring the Whore or composing a song; in either case, he was not forthcoming with explanations.

"And you pleasure them by dancing and singing and—"

"What have you." The blond young man whom Pepy had met in his dream had joined Immortelle in the room, wafting out of her pendant like smoke from an incense jar. Smooth though decidedly not feminine, he looked like a scribe or a flutist, but one who could defend himself against a river man. Pepy begrudged sharing Immortelle with anybody except Harkhuf, but he liked her friend, the young man was so convivial, so uncomplaining about his condition. Though Pepy himself was a man of action, he could appreciate Studs like Tutu—was that the word?—and dreamers like Tike.

"I've heard that phrase before, but nobody has told me what it means. I expect we have a language barrier."

"You might call it the Earthly Paradise. Like this—"

"Tutu," chided Immortelle. "Pepy is too young for such an exhibition."

"Too young! Why, he must be all of twelve! Isn't it time he learned that some things are more fun than leap-cricket or draughts?"

"Still, Harkhuf tells me he isn't ready to hear of such things. Being Pharaoh and all, he must stick to matters of state."

"A virgin at twelve," sighed Tutu. "Some of his best years wasted—the intuitive years, one could say. Why, soon he will grow a beard; Immortelle, it lies with you —your race, your skill, your pride, your tradition, *our* traditions—to set things straight in spite of Harkhuf's prudery."

"Prudery? Harkhuf says. . . ."

"Harkhuf says. . . . Harkhuf says. . . . My dear, one would think you had fallen in love with him." He might have said, "Caught a demon of plague from him."

"Oh, Tutu," she wailed. "It's true, it's true. I am sick, my friend. Sick unto death. Possessed by a demon of love. I have betrayed my profession."

"Minikins *never* fall in love with members of other races," said Tutu with shock and incredulity. It was easy to see his kinship with Immortelle. A subtle spider had woven their golden hair; Hathor had sculptured their features and shaped their limbs to please and dusted their skins with pollen from saffron crocuses. (But who had given them wills like unyielding brass instead of pliable gold? The obverse of love, which Pepy recognized without understanding, jealousy?) "It simply isn't done. It is so unprofessional. Even when we attain the heights of our profession and retire, it is only each other we love. With whom we live. With whom we beget. Must I remind you of such elementary matters? Offer a prayer to Athtar, the Lord of Love, to forgive your waywardness."

"Kiss 'er again, will you?" asked Tike, forgetting the bed and the flute.

Tutu kissed her and held her and hugged her until he almost appeared to solidify; in return, her arms seemed to grapple flesh instead of mist; you could barely see the light through his splendid form. He had grown translucent, not transparent, like an image of jasper in front of a candelabrum. "Don't you still love me, Immortelle?"

"Yes. But I love Harkhuf too. In a different way."

"Is it because I lack the wherewithal? In my present state, don't you know. I thought I had started to make some progress."

"You have, my dear. You have. The wherewithal will return, have no fear."

"What then? He's a big blustering bully, that's what he is, and the way he mistreated his wife Ti is scandalous. Yes, scandalous. Also, the matter of the crocodiles arouses suspicion, to say the least."

"I see that you and Ti have been talking behind my back. Kas and jinns are much more ambulatory than I suspected. She was a *termagant*. She nagged and chided and earned every last crocodile, to say nothing of a hippopotamus or two."

"She began as a dutiful wife, and Harkhuf made her whatever she was to become, possibly a scold but not a termagant. I will *not* have you love such a man."

"But I do love him, Tutu. I'm sick. I have already told you. I love him because he thinks of himself as a roughneck like his father, the farmer, but he has built a secret place in his heart, like the nest of a wren, where he hides his unselfish thoughts. For example, loving Pepy. Pepy, he's like a father to you, isn't he?"

"A second father," said Pepy with pride and affection, but loyal to Pepy I, whom even Harkhuf could never surpass or match. "And protector too. When I called to him in my dream, he came to me all the way from Yam."

"You ask why I love him, Tutu. Because he thinks he looks like a wolf, acts like a wolf, but he's really a gentle bear."

"You have given me reasons, but none convincing."

"Kiss 'er again and 'ug 'er too," said Tike. "Tight. Like a bear."

"What do you know about bears?" asked Pepy. "I never saw one. There isn't a one in Egypt, as far as I know. In the reign of Narmer, hunters killed them for rugs and robes."

"I know by the sound of the name. A wolf's strong

and 'e sneaks. A bear's strong too, but 'e only bites 'is enemies."

"Like a bear," smiled Tutu, repeating his hug. "We have them on Sappharine. Black, brown, spotted, piebald, cinnamon—name the color and I can name the bear."

"All these bears are not to the point," said Immortelle. "There's another reason I love him. (By the way your hugs are improving. Ti should be pleased.) He doesn't love *me*. You see, I am weary of being loved. 'Immortelle, I would like to sip honey from the chalice of your lips.' 'Immortelle, I would like to devour the apples of your breasts.' Always the same compliments, and some of them even sincere. But Harkhuf never compliments me for anything. A mere little dancing girl—that's what I am to him. Isn't it, Pepy?"

"Yes. But then, you do dance—"

"Oh, he uses my body—he has his masculine needs all right. But lovemaking to him is rather like using a water closet."

"For shame," cried Tutu, whitening like a papyrus scroll in the sun. "I never took you for one of those women who like abuse. In *our* profession, there isn't room for such. You shock me beyond speech."

"Then please shut up. No, I don't like abuse. But he is the first man to challenge my arts."

"And if you should break him to your will?"

"Harkhuf isn't breakable. If I should win him, though, I would love him more, not less."

"Well," said Pepy, "if he treats you like a mere little dancing girl, and you aren't going to show us 'What Have You,' why not dance?"

"But she's already shown us," said Tike. "Didn't you see 'ow they kissed? Not like a brother and sister at all. Their lips seemed to nibble each other. There was a business of tongues too." (Sharp-eyed Tike! Dreamers, it seemed, could see as clearly as realists when they chose.) "Don't you understand, Pepy? We 'ave just seen the 'ole thing! Immortelle dances. Sings. Then kisses Tutu in a kind of a 'ungry way, and the next thing you know, she 'as a baby."

"Are you going to have a baby?" asked Pepy with horror and disbelief. "Lose your looks? Swell like a coconut? Forget how to dance?"

"No, Pepy," she smiled, drawing the child into a sweet maternal embrace which included a kiss on his cheek but not his mouth (and not, thank Hathor, the least hint of a nibble).

"I think babies are very agreeable. And mothers too. But not before they are separated, if you know what I mean. I am too low in my profession to have a baby. But when I retire, I expect to have several."

"'As it to do with the number of nibbles?" asked Tike.

"Or the versatility of the tongue?" asked Pepy. "I've heard of a man planting his seed. Does Tutu plant his seed with his tongue, like a farmer his corn from a basket?"

"It isn't that simple. It takes a bit of ploughing as well. Harkhuf, I'm sure, will tell you in good time."

"Well then," said Pepy, "now we know 'What Have You,' and I must say I would rather not have it. But we still haven't seen you dance."

"If she isn't going to dance," muttered Tike, "maybe we could get some sleep."

"Perhaps," continued Pepy, "I could help Harkhuf to fall in love with you. Not that I would insist on a dance in return. But I might feel more inspired to plead your case."

"And I'll play my flute," offered Tike, "if you'll just get on with it."

"Tutu," asked Immortelle. "Will I be prostituting myself if I merely dance?"

"No," said Tutu after a thoughtful pause. "After all, you are dedicated to pleasing men, and if they want a dance, and nothing more, why, then, I say dance. Besides, it may help you to get your mind off Harkhuf. If you don't mind, I'll dance too. I've gotten a cramp from your pendant. Ti, do you care to materialize?"

Materialized, she had the look of belonging beside him; at least, of liking the position. She had lost the sullenness which, like an unbecoming wig, she had worn in Pepy's dream.

"I dance too," she said. "I daresay a Babylonian princess is as carefully trained in the arts of womanhood as a Houri."

"Tutu and I first," said Immortelle. "One of us ought to be solid."

"I am learning to grow more solid like Tutu."

"You have a lot to learn. I can still see right through you."

So it was that Tike played, and Pepy, knowing the tune, sang, and Tutu and Immortelle danced in a boat on a lake beside the Nile, in the land of forbidden magic, the land of Yam. A leopard roared in the demon-haunted dark, craving no doubt the boats and their savory crews. The river dragged its course, like a languorous crocodile, between verdurous banks where oryxes drank with ostriches. Tomorrow is time for the jungle, Pepy thought. Lions and Green Lotuses and Black Dwarves. The question whose answer can spare my kingdom from drought. Tomorrow is time for oracles. Now is tonight. Enchantment lies in the tent.

Once he started to play, Tike resembled a godling instead of a fisherboy. His thin brown limbs became suffused with light. You expected wings to sprout at his shoulder blades. "Stay!" you wanted to cry. "Play for us mortals beneath the immortal moon."

And Pepy sang as silverly as the flute:

ASK THE WIND

Love is an egret's
White cockade.
Why do the feathers
Thin and fade?
Ask the wind.

Love is a lotus'
Bending hall.
Why do the ivory
Ramparts fall?
Ask the wind;

The wily wind
Whose going away
Says only earthen
Things can stay.
Ask the wind.

They circled each other like wary fighters, the solid gold and translucent gold, capturing fire from the lamps; adding fire to their own inherent flames; round and round, circle narrowing, hands reaching, to clasp instead of strike, bodies meeting, to cling instead of crush; dancers, not fighters; lovers; fiery spirits conjured by music and words.

Gold welded with gold; flame united with flame;

indivisible they seemed; hypnotic; at last, dizzying.

"Please," cried Pepy, breaking his song. "You have made me—drunk." Drunk was not the word. He did not know the word. Pharaoh, briefly a man, briefly confronted by feelings beyond his ken, retreated into a child.

"Ah," sighed Immortelle. "We lost ourselves in the dance. Forgive us, Pepy."

"I thought you were going to dance yourselves right out of the tent," said Tike. "Right into the river with the fish."

"I thought it was *disgusting*," said Ti, staring at Tutu, the absence of loincloth, the saffron skin, smooth though stretched above solid flesh, the yellow flame of his hair. Sullenness had returned to her face.

Pepy could understand how Harkhuf had tired of her. *And he wed her when she was only a girl. Eleven years with a pout. A Henna with looks.* Then, before he could start to pity her and be disloyal to his friend, he said to Immortelle, "I'll keep my promise. *Order* Harkhuf to fall in love with you. He can't refuse a pharaoh's command."

"No," she sighed. "Orders are useless in love. You have to be devious, you have to connive and coax."

"Pharaoh is supposed to know everything, but I must have been over-sheltered. I shall just have to feel my way. I can always adopt him, you know. And tell him I need a mother who knows how to dance."

"Harkhuf would as soon marry a crocodile," said Ti. "Sooner. He has a special fondness for the beast."

"Hope is a loyal friend. Expectation a dreamer and fool," said Immortelle.

"Did you make that up yourself?" asked Pepy. "It sounds very sad."

"It's the ultimate law of love. It isn't sad, it's true."

"Does it apply to you and Harkhuf?"

"To everyone, Pepy."

"We shall have to teach some sense to Expectation."

"After we speak to Nilus."

"Oh yes, he must come first, of course. Is he a friendly god?"

"Indifferent, the Minikins say. Sometimes dangerous. You have to plan your approach. You have to know when to speak and when to keep your silence."

"And if you don't?"

"He drowns you and feeds you to the fish."

Chapter VIII

It seemed to Harkhuf that he did not completely, comfortably sleep at any time through the night. Just as his eyelids drooped and his hard muscles, tensed from the day's activities, relaxed into ease, the deep-throated cry of a goatsucker startled him upright on his couch; then the trumpet-bird, recalling battle charges and Babylonians; then a stridulation of starlings, swallows, guinea-fowl, parrots. . . . Clearly, the place was a paradise for birds; he wished for a bow and arrows.

"Merciful Hathor," he swore. "How can a man get his sleep with such a racket?" He envisioned a stew of birds, spiced appropriately with onions, garlic, and vinegar.

But Harkhuf had slept through earthquakes and sandstorms. Explorer and warrior, he was accustomed to sleep in any place, at any time; in a canopied bed or on hard, wet ground. Something besides the birds had disturbed his night.

Was he afraid of the morning, the Nile, the oracle of the god?

Afraid of the morning, yes, but surely not of confronting a river god or of learning a secret which might avert a drought. In Egypt, oracles were as commonplace as temples, even if not in rivers.

Afraid, yes. Of—what? The question seemed to him unanswerable. The fear seemed to him indecipherable. He did not like to think, he liked to act.

Still, as long as he could not sleep. . . .

To most Egyptians, other races were either different and inferior or similar and inferior. Harkhuf liked to think of the Cretans as gifted but childlike; the Babylonians as dour and guilt-ridden, the builders of architectural atrocities called ziggurats; and the Bedouins as beneath contempt except in war. Everyone not Egyptian was categorized as a Foreigner and dismissed, disdained, or patronized. But the Minikins forced him to now comparisons. They built well, even if boats instead of houses; they battled the Black Dwarves, a foe as deadly as Bedouins, they worshipped grace and beauty but they were as strong as they were beautiful, and littleness in them was hardly quaintness. In a phrase, they were not barbarians.

Furthermore, they were kinsmen of Immortelle.

Immortelle was a Whore. She flaunted the fact, as a lady of Egypt might flaunt her kinship to Pharaoh. The Brown Minikins, however, treated her like a visiting princess. She who had seemed a decorative trifle had guided ferocious rocs, planned the rescue of Pepy, returned him, along with Tike, to Aquamarine, and arranged for the meeting with the river god. The whores he had known had been trained to pleasure men. Harkhuf preferred them to ladies. But for matters weightier than pleasure, he looked to his followers, Dedwen and his Nubians, Egyptian bowmen.

The truth was plain: Immortelle was more than an object of pleasure. Like Ti, willful and stubborn, she accomplished tasks to baffle a man; unlike Ti, she never raised her voice.

Immortelle was unique, Immortelle was. . . . He had never been good at addition.

"Harkhuf, old man," he swore. "You're overrating the wench. She's exactly what she said. A whore, though much the best in your unlimited experience. A sleepless night breeds sickly fancies."

Perhaps if he closed his eyes and tried to ignore the birds. Or threw a rock. . . .

"It is time to visit the oracle," said Immortelle, entering the room in a topless and almost bottomless garment which could only be likened to the abbreviation of a Cretan bull dancer. "You see, I am ready for a swim." When he gaped at her physical ornaments . . . breasts . . . nipples . . . uhmmmmm . . . when he sniffed her musk, she continued, "At the risk of offending your modesty, I suggest that you wear nothing at all. The river appears to be sluggish; it holds, however, treacherous currents. Rings, pectorals, even those voluminous loincloths you Egyptians wear—they will only encumber you."

"Offend my modesty?" he protested. "I'll have you know our farmers till their fields—naked. My father was a farmer, as I have said. Temple dancers dance in nothing but rings and anklets. My mother danced in a temple to Hathor before she married my father." To prove his point, he sprang to the floor and flaunted his ungirt masculinity.

Much to his surprise, he felt a sense of shame. Yet he had felt no shame when he had made love to her in the cave of Ganesh.

She took his hand. "We can let the boys sleep. They were much more tired than they realized. And Pepy has borne a terrible strain for a long, long time now. Since his father died."

"I've been like a father to him."

"I know," she said, "and he loves you dearly. From a distance. You rarely linger at court . . ."

"I went to Yam to get him a dancing dwarf, didn't I?"

"You went because you wanted to go. 'Go,' I repeat. If it hadn't been to Yam for a dwarf, it would have been to Crete to wrestle the bulls, or to Punt for apes and ivory."

Harkhuf detested women who were right; Ti had often been right. Dislike for Immortelle flickered briefly across his mind, like a bumblebee, but soon disappeared into a flower. She knew how to tell the truth without reproach.

The Brown Minikins were awake with the birds. There are towns which at night assume the misty allurements of a dream but by day become drab and colorless in the blanching sun, or squalid with beggars and filth. Not Aquamarine. The boats were inverted rainbows gleaming opalescently in the pale green waters. The twisting jetties were dragons with many-colored scales. Everywhere, people had started to work, bundling papyrus reeds to repair a cabin, swimming between the boats with filmy nets on wooden rods to capture fish, yes, even carving boomerangs out of the ivory tusks of the elephants whose trumpetings resounded across the lake.

Something sidled against his legs.

"Anubis," he swore, "a leopard!"

"A civet cat," smiled Immortelle. "Minikins love animals and these are practical as well as beautiful. Minikin traders scratch the musky secretions from their pouches, collect them in hollow horns from dead

oxen, and make a perfume to trade with the Black
Dwarves—that is to say, in times of peace—for the
produce of the jungle, lianas, bananas, baobob wood,
etc." Spotted, whiskered, with long thick tails, the
cats were as long as the Minikins were tall, but they
sidled among their masters with good-humored con-
descension. Like most of their race, they agreed to
become pets in return for the benefits of a regular
diet—in this case, porridge and milk—and the protection of undemanding masters, but they kept both their
dignity and their independence and disappeared into
the jungle whenever they chose to mate or forage for
meat denied them by the Minikins.

"You're sure they only forage in the jungle?" asked
Harkhuf, eyeing a cat which was eyeing him as if he
were next week's dinner.

"He likes you," said Immortelle.

"I see he does. And my roc liked me too, didn't she?
Just where is she now?"

"No one ever knows where they go when they
want to be alone. The two are lovers, you see. But
when I call them, believe me, they will come.

"Now then, Avram here will guide us. Avram, meet
Harkhuf."

A young man had parted the rushes in the door.

"You realize," continued Immortelle, "that I am a
visitor just like you, Harkhuf. I don't even know my
way to the oracle. Avram knows the jungle and also
the current in the river."

As naked as Harkhuf, Avram appeared to be small
only when you took the time to measure his scant
four feet in height. Otherwise, he gave the illusion of
size and strength. His skin was tautly stretched across
muscle and bone, but he seemed more graceful than
gaunt, and more powerful than graceful. He moved

like the surefooted panther instead of the nimble
gazelle. His skin was as brown as a coconut, but as
right for him as saffron for Immortelle. Harkhuf
looked at him fixedly to judge his intention toward
Immortelle. Had he spent the night with her? His
Holy Rod was totally disproportionate to his height; it
was, in fact, worthy of Min, the phallic god, and Harkhuf resisted the urge to reach for a loincloth. However, the look between the Brown Minikin and the
Golden Minikin appeared to be camaraderie and not
desire.

"Nothing to fear from the animals," Avram reas-
sured Harkhuf, shaking his boomerang. "Even a leopard is afraid of this. But the god is another matter. We
don't often ask him questions. He is old and—well, like
the river, moody."

"We'll hope for a gracious mood," said Harkhuf.
"Should we take him a gift?"

"We'll be lucky if we get ourselves to his cave,
much less gifts. No, there's nothing he wants unless
we could carry him a fetching virgin, but Minikins
are too small for him. He's a giant, you see. Tall as
a kapok tree."

"And even a Whore," explained Immortelle, "is not
that adaptable."

"He has drowned three Minikins in the last year.
You're a good swimmer, aren't you, Harkhuf?" His
mouth seemed made to smile, but sympathy sobered
his tone and his countenance.

"Oh, yes." It was true. Harkhuf had swum in the
Nile as a boy and dived with hippopotami.

"Well then, we're off."

The Nile was neither noble nor beautiful at this
particular season, before it had started to rise. In fact,

explained Avram, it should have already risen from the innumerable tributaries, lakes, and mountains of melting snow to the South. Clearly, Nilus had delayed the rise of the water; clearly the god was angry with Egypt. His river resembled a huge dead crocodile affronting the brightnesses of baobob trees as plump as cedars and much more luxuriant, the opalescent bloom of the protea vine bedecking jungle copses like the robes of ceremonial dancers, the tree veronica tunneling green labyrinths where monkeys hid from panthers. It sounded particularly dead when you heard baboons, those little moving earthquakes, snort through the trees; or the fiery-feathered parrots squawk like clashing sistrums.

Clumps of papyrus drifted aimlessly from bank to bank; dead white ants littered the water like numberless flakes of manna.

"But remember the current. There," said Avram, adventure twinkling in his eyes; young eyes in the face of a man the size of a boy (except for his endowment); young thoughts but tempered with mature precautions. Harkhuf trusted him. A clump of papyrus erupted into life; spurted, twisted, dipped, bobbled below the surface like a float on a line which has caught a fish.

"The cave of Nilus is protected by that current. He makes it himself, of course."

"He urinates," said Immortelle without any show of embarrassment. "Or so I am told."

"Not all the time," laughed Avram. "Other times, I expect he just conjures it out of the earth in the fashion of gods. Anyway, he's a crotchety old fellow. He likes his privacy."

"Won't he overhear you?" Gods of course could

overhear mortals whenever they chose, even river gods in subterranean caves.

"If he wanted to. But he won't be bothered. He'd rather sleep or—well, I'd better not give away all of his secrets, or he might decide to listen after all and drown me."

Avram waded carefully into the water, holding to Immortelle, and she in turn held tightly to Harkhuf with her four small fingers. Her hand, however, did not belong to a whore. It was a hand of bronze.

"Once in the water," said Avram, "it will be impossible to keep together. The water is too murky, and the current will jerk us under from time to time. But head for the opposite bank. Then hold your breath and dive and look for a large triangular opening just about your height below the surface. Keep diving till you find it. That's the door to his cave."

Why, there isn't any current at all, thought Harkhuf. The Nile is as still as the lake of Chemmis! Once he got used to the salty taste of the water, he concentrated on watching Immortelle ahead of him, gold and pellucid like the Sirens from the Great Green Sea; flickering forever, it seemed, minutely out of his reach.

The current hit him like a physical counterpart to the Green Melancholy.

Dazed, breathless, slipping into the maelstrom of sleep or death, he thought of Immortelle. . . . He did not want to climb the Celestial Ladder, unless there were whores in Paradise.

He awoke in the cave of the god. A triangle opening from the river . . . a pool . . . a bank . . . a forest of giant mushrooms: parasols, blobs, cones, glittering orange and red in the strange light which emanated from the roof and the walls (he could not see the furthest wall because of the mushrooms, some of them taller than palm trees). Immortelle and Avram were kneeling beside him and holding his hands.

"I thought you could swim," said Avram, with affectionate reproach.

"I can," snapped Harkhuf, angry at having had to be rescued by anyone, particularly someone half his size; particularly *two* someones. But a look at Immortelle and he forgot his anger. She looked like a ka. Concern had drained her of gold.

She squeezed his hand with reassurance. "Avram, I think he swam very well. After all, he's never met such a current."

"Neither have you, but you helped me drag him into the cave."

"But I'm a Minikin."

"True," said Avram, "and he's only an Egyptian."

"We build *indestructible* pyramids," said Harkhuf.

"You do indeed," smiled Avram. "I didn't mean to make light of your achievements. Only your inexperience in foreign lands with foreign gods."

Harkhuf, the explorer, struggled to swallow his pride—it was hard, what with the water in his stomach. "I guess I'm indebted to both of you."

"Think nothing of it. Where would Immortelle and I be in a sandstorm?"

"*Will you please skip the amenities and get the Hell out of my cave?*" Hell to Egyptians was an absence of the Celestial Paradise, an eternal bodiless wandering in the Red Desert. The oath was as frightening as the bellow.

They did not see the god behind his forest of mushrooms; they never saw the god, though Harkhuf caught a hoary white glimpse among the reds and oranges. *Beard no doubt. By Set's Unholy Rod, it's as big as a tent.*

"Beloved Nilus," said Avram.

"Let the Lady talk," snapped the god.

"Remember his titles," whispered Avram, and Immortelle resumed the questioning.

"Almighty One, Lord of the Nile, Prophet, Seer, and Magus, Ancient of Days, we have come to ask your counsel," she said, facing the voice and speaking with clear if daintily feminine tones.

"You Minikins do very well on your own. Why ask me?"

"I am asking for the sake of my Egyptian friend and his people."

"I don't like Egyptians. I only flood their fields because they build temples to me and sacrifice bulls when I take a mind to swim north."

"I am asking for the sake of the man I love."

Large, bleary eyes peered through the mushrooms. Sleepy eyes. It was hard to distinguish them from round, red mushrooms.

"The *Egyptian?*"

"Yes, oh venerable Nilus."

"Other one's better endowed." ("Damn," muttered Harkhuf. "What does he expect after a cold swim?") "Still, it's your choice. You're a pretty little piece. Spunky too. I like you. Pity you're not a mite larger. Might have some fun. Don't let this white beard fool you. I still know how to frolic. Well, go ahead and ask your question. Make it brief, though. You've already ruined my nap."

"Is Egypt due for a drought?"

"In other words, am I going to hold back some of my water?"

"Exactly."

"Yes."

"Yes?" It was Harkhuf's first contribution to the dialogue.

"Yes."

"Can you tell us why, esteemed and holy one?" Immortelle.

"Ask the Green Lotus."

"But Honorable Nilus—"

Further questions were greeted first by snorts, then a loud snore. The three questioners turned to each other in mutual dismay.

"The Lotus was there before I was born," said Avram. "It was there when my ancestors came from Sappharine. But it hasn't always been—hurtful."

"I've been *in* the flower," said Harkhuf.

"Truly?" asked Avram with surprise and respect.

"And it almost killed me."

"I'm not surprised. Nobody else even goes close."

"I thought it might have something to do with the ka of my ex-wife, Ti, who was eaten by crocodiles and for some reason holds a grudge against me."

"Oh? We don't have kas in Yam, we have jinns."

"Like Tutu," said Immortelle.

"But they can be nasty if they choose."

"Unlike Tutu."

"They tend to hold grudges."

"I know what you mean. Anyway, I questioned Ti and didn't learn a thing. That's not to say that she doesn't have something to do with it. She's a sly one, like most Babylonians."

"What do you suggest?"

"I'll just have to try again."

"DON'T."

"And why, by Hathor's Holy Nipples, not?" Harkhuf was so aggravated—everybody, it seemed, was

saving his life, speaking for him, giving him orders—
that he forgot the god's titles.

"Send Pepy and Tike."

"Two little boys?" cried Harkhuf.

"Send Pepy and Tike."

A snort and then a snore.

Chapter IX

It was a bewildered army—Pepy and Tike, Tutu and Ti, Harkhuf and Immortelle—which gathered beneath the doubtful protection of a tree veronica, swirling a leafy dome above their heads. Advance or retreat or stand their ground? The answer lay with the Lotus faintly visible to the south. Did the bronze-green foliage above them disport in a wind unfelt on the ground or writhe in the melancholy of its gigantic sister, the Lotus?

Sunburned Harkhuf looked as pale as the ivory in a Minikin boomerang. Immortelle seemed somehow—quenched—like a lamp of alabaster caught in a sudden draught. Tutu and Ti, who appeared to be holding hands, had never looked more immaterial, more nearly invisible without actually disappearing from view. Tike had the look of a boy who has missed a meal. Only Pepy was reasonably confident. For he was going about his business as Pharaoh; going to save his country from drought; and performing a duty always gave him confidence.

"I can't let you go," said Harkhuf as if he were barking an order to his men. "I went the other time. Escaped by myself. I'll go again."

"But the flower almost killed you," Pepy reminded him.

"Almost isn't altogether."

"Dear friend Harkhuf, why visit an oracle if you don't take his advice? Nilus wanted Tike and me to go. You said so yourself."

"He's a senile old man."

"He's also a giant," said Immortelle, "and he does control the Nile." The illusion of height she sometimes projected, the sheer power of her will, had dissipated beneath the tree veronica. She looked like a child, not a coward to be sure, but awed and minimized with apprehension.

"You want them to go, don't you, Immortelle?" snapped Harkhuf. "It was you who led us to that confounded oracle. You and your friend Avram. And you suggested the oracle in the first place, back in Egypt."

"I do *not* want them to go," she said, staring Harkhuf angrily in the eye. "I love them like the sons I am not yet allowed to have. But Nilus isn't a monster, whatever his moods. He must have had his reasons."

"Anyway, I'm going," said Pepy, placing a protective arm over Tike's shoulder. "Tike must decide for himself."

"I'm going too," stammered Tike. "I want to climb that l-ladder."

"No," snapped Harkhuf.

"Pharaoh goes where he chooses, and takes whom he chooses," Pepy reminded his friend. He did not raise his voice, but copper rang in his words. "Besides, I'm not even hurting from the flower. I just feel a sort of tingle. And you, little friend Tike?"

"A sort of 'unger. But it doesn't 'urt either, except in the pit of my stomach, and Immortelle 'as promised to 'ave a dinner waiting for us when we get back. Beef would be fine," he suggested, then, remembering his company, hurried to add, "though fish will do nicely."

"You mean you don't feel the pain?" cried Harkhuf.

"Immortelle feels it. I can see it in her face. Don't you, Immortelle?"

"Yes. It's like being prodded with darts."

He moved swiftly to encircle her with his arms. The gesture was more than repentance for his rudeness, and Pepy watched them with pleasure—his two dearest friends—but also an unaccountable hurt which he quickly trotted out of his mind, like a mischievous sphinx.

"And you, Tutu? Ti?"

The jinn and the ka were as silent as the wind. They had obliterated into invisibility, and, if one could judge by their silence, departed from the dome. Harkhuf looked at his ring, Immortelle at her pendant of sapphire stars.

"I think they are really gone," said Harkhuf. "I don't feel a prickle under the stone."

"Tutu is so tenderhearted he couldn't wait around to see the boys off."

"Ti must have had a different reason," said Harkhuf. "Except for Tutu, I expect she would have hurried them on their way."

"At least," said Immortelle, "the boys don't hurt. Nilus knew exactly what he was saying. The Lotus is opening a path for them but not for us. Almost an invitation."

"Or a trap," said Harkhuf darkly. "She may want to get them into her lair."

"Flowers don't 'ave lairs," said Tike, who loved a daisy as much as a cousin. "Spiders build lairs *in* or *among* or *under* flowers."

"This flower has a lair. And she eats little boys. Yes, eats them just like a spider with two tasty fireflies."

"Well," said Pepy, resisting Harkhuf's attempt to frighten him out of the journey, "a flower that big won't get much nourishment out of a pharaoh of twelve. If she were going to eat someone, I would think she would have eaten you." Vaguely he wondered why he thought of the flower as a "she." Because of the cradle beside the canopied bed? Because of Harkhuf's intimation that Ti was involved with the flower? Still, "she" might be a "he" or an "it" or even a "them." Pepy envisioned a cradle inhabited by "their" spawn, a spider, a sphinx, a goose-necked sta.

"She'll get indigestion from me," said Tike. "I'm tough."

"Pitcher plants dissolve their prey in a sticky secretion," said Harkhuf. "Tough or not."

"I promise, we won't get stuck," said Pepy.

"The Black Dwarves. What about them? For all we know, they live in the flower just as they do in kapok trees."

With such encouragement, Pepy and Tike began a journey which might prove deadlier than a ride on the back of an irascible roc, or more beneficial to Egypt than repelling a host of temple-toppling barbarians.

Thus they began the journey of their lives.

"There isn't any ladder," sighed Tike.

The boys stared in consternation at a stem as large as the trunk of a cedar from Lebanon, at the smooth green petals flaring above them like an impregnable fortress. "I've climbed the trees in Egypt. Date palms and tamarisks. When I was a little boy, I even worked with the monkeys to pick some figs in the top of a tree. I can shinny up a trunk without any branches. But a stem is something else. There aren't any knots for 'and 'olds, and it's too big around to 'ug."

"Peduncle."

"What do your relatives 'ave to do with climbing a stem?"

" 'Peduncle' is the proper name for stem."

"Please, Pepy, don't talk like a pharaoh. We've business at 'and. I suggest—"

Tike, it seemed, was about to usurp Pepy's function. The helpless dreamer was proving himself intolerably practical.

"*There*," said Pepy, desperate for an answer.

The answer was the opening at the foot of the stem; straight sides, rounded top; in fact, a small but carefully carven door. He pushed Tike behind him, knelt under the lintel, and entered the stem, expecting to meet a leopard, a crocodile, or an angry ka. Doors into giant lotuses surely had their guardians.

The guardian was a sphinx, an adolescent the size of a small lion, though of course the wings suggested a bennu bird, and the tail—well, the tail suggested nothing in Egypt or Nubia. A grapevine covered with mottled fur, he thought. A hawser frayed by many uses in many weathers. It was not a decorative tail, but it snapped and coiled with the mobility of a whip.

"Pepy," said Tike, backing toward the entrance without taking his eyes from the snap of the tail. "We aren't wanted."

"Nonsense. He hasn't lashed us, has he? He's simply warning us to mind our manners."

"I don't 'ave any," said Tike. "I'm an orphan."

"Just keep quiet and do what I do." Pharaoh was in command.

He would not have been surprised to find a ladder or circular stairway, so obviously were they meant to enter and ascend the tower of living greenery. (Or be devoured by the guardian sphinx.) Failing to discover such man-made conveniences, he quickly noted that the walls were soft and mushy, with hard projections which would serve for hand- and-footholds.

"Can you make it, Tike? Or would you rather wait—?"

Tike had already begun to climb the wall and Pepy was pressed to overtake him and reassert his position. The sphinx sat on its haunches and stared at them from the floor, lashing its tail. Forgoing the usual inscrutability of the beast, it looked satisfied, as if it knew what awaited the boys; it looked expectant, as if it meant to devour them if they were not devoured by the flower. It was rather like a dog which lurks under the table for its master to throw it a bone: faithful, grateful, and hungry.

"I learned to climb when I was three," said Tike, peering down at the sphinx. "My father was a sailor, you see, and 'e took me on a voyage and I climbed the mast every day to see all the monsters and Sirens. . . ."

Pepy was more concerned with monsters at hand. "Hush," he said, "something may be listening."

"Well, obviously the flower is listening. 'Asn't she invited us in? And I wouldn't be surprised if that animal down there 'eard every word we said. Did you notice the size of its ears? Big as an elephant's. But if we talk, we won't 'ave to 'ear it 'owl."

"That's not the sphinx, that's something else." It was like the sound of the wind as it whirls in little eddies over the desert and then, angry at finding no friends in all that barren space, explodes into a tremendous funnel and looks for enemies.

Side by side, Pepy perhaps a trifle higher for the sake of decorum, they climbed the stem, as one may climb the wall of a cliff where tough roots alternate with soft leaves or patches of treacherous sand. There was no discernible outer source of light, only the pale green glow from the walls, but they could glimpse the tunnel above them, tall and straight, the very heart of the stem; a tunnel for carrying sap from the roots to the leaves and petals; empty now like a dry river-bed (emptied now for the two boys?). With each upward climb, Pepy felt more—awaited—but whether as guest or prisoner, he did not know, nor want to know. A fear had settled upon him like subtle sap, less of a threat to his life than to his mind, a truth more terrible than a lie.

"We must be near a nectary," he said at last.

"If you mean the place smells like a 'orehouse, you're right," said Tike, and the boys exchanged expectant and happy looks, because they were surely nearing the top of the stem and because their acquaintance with whores had left them with unqualified admiration. (Whores had sheltered Tike on lonely nights. Immortelle was a whore. Where was the lady with such compassion and grace? Henna? The only tolerable part of her was her wig, because it hid her hair. Ti? A dour expression and a wagging tongue.)

"And there through that little hole—door. I believe it's the chamber Harkhuf talked about. It must be the ovary."

"That's where babies are grown in a woman," said Tike with the worldly expression of one who has lived in the streets.

"I wouldn't know about that. I always thought Hathor slipped them into a woman's stomach while she slept."

"Oh, no. A 'ore I knew—she used to let me sleep in 'er 'ut—said a physician tied her ovaries so she wouldn't 'ave babies to tie up 'er business."

"What do babies have to do with business?"

"I expect they snuffle when a gentleman comes to

call," said Tike with the wistful note of one whose only voyages had been with an imaginary father.

"She was just telling you a tale," said Pepy, who thought it improper for a pharaoh to learn such intimacies from a fisherboy, even a friend. Actually, he had always suspected the story about Hathor. With such an occupation, she would never have time to rest in fertile Egypt, and everyone knew that she liked to sing and dance or take her ease (with a god) on a couch of flaxen coverlets. "You know how physicians are. They use a lot of big words to impress us and make us pay big fees, a calf to pull a tooth or six honeycombs to cure an earache. 'Trepanning' and words like that."

"Well, anyway, we seem to be in the ovary," said Tike, looking around him for babies and finding a bed. "You know, I'm sleepy as well as 'ungry."

"And I'm starting to hurt. The tingle has turned into a burn. Tike, I said—" It was highly unflattering to have a fisherboy fall asleep in the middle of your sentence, but Tike had climbed into the bed, like a baby waiting to be born (that is, if you could trust the physician's tale), and closed his eyes.

"Tike," cried Pepy, "it isn't your bed. A visitor never goes to sleep in a stranger's house without an invitation!"

No amount of nudging, not even a forceful prod, could budge him from his nap.

"Oh, well, maybe they do in whorehouses."

He looked around him and studied the ovary, the room which Harkhuf had described in terrifying detail, the brazier, changing color like an angry hippopotamus, the cradle which somehow looked like a mouth, and he wanted to join Tike in the bed and pull the covers over his head or, since the bed resembled a larger mouth, awaken Tike and slither down the stem and, detouring the sphinx, hurry to Aquamarine and Harkhuf and Immortelle.

He had started to hurt in earnest. He felt as if he had burst into flames like a hayrick in the Nubian sun.

But he stood his ground in the fashion of his father.

"My lady Lotus," he called. Every lady, every person, from Pharaoh to the lowliest peasant, must be addressed by a name or a title. It was a custom older than Egypt. It did not seem strange to him to use the name of a flower. "Immortelle" was also the name of a flower; "Henna," that of a plant. "I am Pepy II, Pharaoh of Egypt, fourth king (not counting a regent when I was small), Sixth Dynasty." (Among strangers, he felt it proper and prudent to identify his country and describe his lineage. Among strangers, "Egypt" generally implied a combination of power, wisdom, and wealth, and "Pharaoh" was thought to own everything including his people.) "Nilus sent me your message and I've come to visit you with my friend Tike." Then, after a decorous pause, "And I also want to ask you a very important question."

He began to feel foolish; he began to sweat and smart and ache. How could a Green Lotus answer a human boy?

The Lotus found a way.

He seemed to see the earth as if from the back of a roc, the Delta marshes, and voices came to his ears, muted as if from a great distance, recognizable like the speakers. . . .

"Harkhuf, I must say you astonished me when you suggested a picnic on the river." The speaker was Ti. The river was not the Nile, it was one of those countless tributaries which meandered among islets with clumps of palm trees: papyrus plants raising their feathery leaves on stalks like the fans of fashionable ladies; lotuses, pink and white and blue, scattered among the fans like so many precious gems from the bountiful hand of Hathor. If not the incomparable river which nourished Egypt, it was at least a rivulet with intimacy, too remote for the fisherboys and the river men, a place for lovers and love's sweet dalliance, espied by none except Ra.

As for Ti—well, the region became her, the region made her bloom. She was rarer than any flower. Wigless, she had allowed her natural hair to fall in soft, russet ringlets over her forehead and onto her petal-white shoulders. Barebreasted in the new Cretan style, she wore a single amethyst on a chain between her breasts, and a flaring skirt like an upturned blossom to match the singular jewel. But it was her face which captivated Pepy. Always, first as a lady in his father's court, later as a ka, she had seemed to wear a mask, beautiful but hard and arrogant. Now, he saw fresh skin and eyes as guileless as Ra's blue sky, and a mouth which trembled into a young girl's smile. He did not want to like her. He was used to her arrogance, her railing at Harkhuf, his friend, her boasting of noble blood and Babylonian luxuries. He was used to pitying his friend.

Sounds reverberated among the silences . . . the bellow and slosh of hippopotami at play . . . the cry of a startled ibis . . . the swish, swish, swish from the oars of the frail canopied boat of papyrus reeds, rowed by four of Harkhuf's own oarsmen and fellow adventurers.

"When else do I have my wife to myself?" asked Harkhuf.

"Whenever you want," sighed Ti, "which is about as often as the rain falls on the Red Desert."

"Now, now, Ti, we mustn't let past differences spoil

our day. I have instructed the cook to prepare us a lunch of coconut cakes and lamprey eels."

"I am not even mistress of my own kitchen. Still, you have chosen well, and I am ravenous. Shall we—"

The boat shuddered and lurched, as if a hippopotamus had shoved the stern. No, it was the oarsmen, plunging their oars as if to a secret command.

"Must we go so fast? Lampreys are indigestible at such a speed."

"Here, give me your hand and I will settle you snugly beside me on my seat. The boatmen are doubtless seeking a quiet nook for our lunch."

Somewhat unsteadily, overweighted by her generous breasts, awkward in her new Cretan gown, bewildered no doubt by Harkhuf's solicitude, the princess Ti attempted to rise to her feet.

"Harkhuf, give me your hand."

"Stretch a little further, my dear. There, our fingers are almost touching."

"Harkhuf!"

"Stretch!"

"Harkhuf. . . ."

"Husband," she wailed through a mouth of water. "You are leaving me behind the boat. And the river is hot and slimy." Her wet and disheveled hair, coppery in the sun, shone like a buoy or beacon.

"There, there, my dear. We have only to make a circle and get you back into the boat. You don't want us to pole backwards and crush you, I trust."

"I don't care how you pole. Just pole." Then—"Something is lurking among the lotuses. Staring at my hair. Staring at *me* as if I were dinner. . . . All I can see is a pair of raised, squinty eyes."

"A harmless waterfowl, no doubt."

"A waterfowl with a snout?"

"Beak perhaps?"

"*Snout.*"

"Undoubtedly it is a crocodile. You have probably frightened him out of a nap. Put on a brave front and he will leave you alone."

"You know I have no front. At your own insistence, I dressed in the Cretan style."

"A pity, my dear. If he spies your bosom, he may want a closer look. It is one of your glories, even after all these years. Your splendor of splendors, if I may use a pharaonic term."

"Harkhuf, he has friends."

"Crocodiles always have friends. A rivulet gets lonely."

"Harkhuf!"

"Patience, my sweet. I will smite them with my staff."

When the boat had completed its turn, there were no crocodiles to smite; alas, there was no Ti.

He made a diligent sweep and recovered her amethyst pendant from a lotus pad. Smoothed, polished, set in a large mount, the stone would adorn his own brown finger.

"Harkhuf!" cried Pepy, wanting an explanation, at least a show of grief; hating his friend and wanting to drive the hurtful and unfamiliar sensation out of his heart, as a farmer dislodges the bees from a hive with a cloud of smoke.

The answer did not come in words.

Burning coals, he thought. I am tumbling over embers and each of them burns me as I turn and turn, and even my hair is insufficient shield, and the pectoral which ought to guard my heart collects and multiplies the burns.

To open his eyes was at once a risk and a need; to
see the embers, avoid the burns. . . .

But he did not see a fire.

He saw a room, a great empty bed whose canopy
seemed to shift and shimmer, as if it were woven by
an Oxyrhynchid, one of those evil spider-crabs which
infested the floor of the Nile and caught the unwary
swimmer in webs like streamers of seaweed and bright
anemones. For what but a mate-devouring spider, a
crab with claws to rend, could lure him into the flower
and stab him with such a multitude of pains? Cruel,
cruel beyond measure, even beyond the forgiveness
of a pharaoh who went among his people, disguised, to
feed the hungry and clothe the naked. . . . He ached
and feared and loathed, and he wished to die and felt
ashamed of the wish.

It came to him like surcease from fire, surcease from
the burning thrust at his heart, that the fire had not
been intended for him; that whatever had seized the
room and hammered the bed and scattered the toys
was enmeshed, like a weaver of webs, in its own in-
tolerable pain. The burns he felt on his body, agonizing but superficial, emanated, flared, exploded in the
heart of the flower or whatever possessed the flower.

Thus did he find the one possible shield:

Pity.

Not an impervious shield; no more impervious than
taut and sun-hardened leather against a well-aimed
Bedouin spear. But better than nakedness. At least he
could breathe; at least he could listen; at least he could
see and try to encompass what he saw. . . .

He seemed to be looking through the green trans-
parencies of a lake. Bed, cradle, brazier faded as if
the current had melted and mingled them with the
sandy floor. Other objects trembled into solidity, but

far . . . far . . . from the flower. There was more than
mist between him and the objects, the houses, the
pylons, the people, there was time like a wall of water.
The dress of the people was much the same as that of
his own subjects, the linen loincloths for the men,
with their copper clasps in the shape of an eye or a
beetle; the ankle-length gowns for the women, their
wigs like clustered black poppies or beehives or
sheaths of wheat. They were unmistakably Egyptian;
still, they were not his subjects. . . .

A sadness gripped them, however, almost a desperation, as in his own time when dreams or phoenixes
prophesied drought. They were threatened, but
whether by injury or loss to themselves he could not
tell, so baffled they seemed, going about their tasks
with the look of dreamers obeying a pharaoh, a god,
a power beyond their resistance or comprehension;
yielding obedience instead of love. His eye, like the
all-seeing eye of Ra, swung from household to household; in every garden, it seemed, the family had
gathered to perform the identical rite. The father was
tilting a gourd and pouring water over an image of
Horus, the falcon-god and slayer of demons; his wife
and children, fearfully, furtively, one at a time, marched
to bathe their hands in the bowl which caught the
water. On the back of every woman or girl, over her
gown, hung a *menyt* sacred to Hathor and bane to
demons, a slender metal rod which bulged at either
end like a breast of the goddess. On the chest of every
man and boy, in the midst of his pectoral, an eye of
Horus, gold, copper, lapis lazuli, depending on the
wealth of the owner, had been hastily implanted,
attached by a metal clasp or stuck with clay, to protect the wearer and stare defiance at enemies.

In the shops of the artisans, a different and much
more difficult ritual was being performed: Potters

were painting symbols on their bowls and platters—of
Set and his minions—and smashing them with a combination of zeal and reluctance into a hundred pieces,
or handing them to men and women who, another
time, would have paid in kind, but snatched at them
now without offering payment, without, it seemed,
being expected to pay, and dashed them onto the
ground, and ground them under their feet as if they
were noxious insects, scorpions or tarantulas. Images
of blue faïence hippopotami had been placed in front
of the shops, and those who entered the portals bowed
before these grotesque but powerful beings, symbols
of luck though clumsy and often destructive in life,
the bane of the river man, the scourge of the swimmer.
Departing, the worshippers hurried to temples flanked
by larger images and breathed the odor of incense as if
it could cleanse their lungs of poisonous vapors and
joined the conjurations of priests to Ra, invoked as
the Bull of the Sky called Wenis, and swayed to the
sound of dancing priestesses before they passed the
pylon gates:

The sky pours water, the stars darken;
The Bows rush about, the bones of the Earth-god
    tremble.
They are still, the Pleiades,
When they see Wenis appearing, animated. . . .
Wenis is the Bull of the sky, who conquers
    according to his desire,
Who lives on the being of every god,
Who eats their entrails, who comes when their
    belly is filled with magic
From the Island of Fire. . . .
It is Wenis who judges with Him whose name is
    hidden
On this day of Slaying the Oldest One. . . . .

The conjurations faded into a cry. At first it seemed the faint and distant buzzing of innumerable locusts, a plague on the wing. It was not a plague; it moved and grew and swelled into a lamentation, as if all of the voices in Egypt were mourning a single death. It was loss, anguish, despair; a royal mummy destroyed by thieves, a pharaoh stabbed in his bed.

EXORCISM.

It was the time of which Pepy's father had written with pride and fear and something behind the words inscribed from right to left by a rush pen in the hand of a royal scribe: the route of the demons from North to South, from Egypt to Yam. But whether the lamentation was that of the demons, or of the people who, even while routing them, feared and mourned their departure, he could not tell. The Red Ones had peopled the land before the coming of the Egyptians, the god Set with the forked tail and white skin and coarse red hair like the pelt of an ass; his companion, Taueret, with the head of a lion and the body of a hippopotamus, and their demoniac crew, makers of mischief, demanding prayers and sacrifices, training magicians in the black arts. Children of the night.

But evil had its opposite. Set could blight the flax or cool the desert with gentle breezes. Taueret could strangle a baby in his mother's womb or ease the mother through a difficult labor. It was the way of magic; good and evil inextricably intertwined, the Seven Imperishable Stars in a black sky. The pattern was older than the earliest mastaba, older than the rise and fall of the Nile, and now it was broken, like a tomb despoiled by thieves, invaded by jackals; like a river dammed and diverted from its predestined course; and cold, merciless reason would rule in a land where thieves had sometimes been kinder than pha-

raohs, and mystery had been an exaltation as well as a
fear. . . .

Then he seemed to enter a chamber of his own
palace at Memphis, but in a time before his remem-
brance, and he saw a woman lying on the bed, young
as Immortelle, still as if in death. So white and perfect
she lay, she might have been carved from ivory. He
had never seen anyone, princess or priestess, so sad or
beautiful. Faded red hair both framed and partly concealed her face; hair which was neither the brilliant
red of the desert in the sun, nor the poppy, turning its
face to Ra at noon; rather of that departing light from
the solar chariot as it rolled below the horizon. A
damp linen robe enveloped her shrunken limbs, though
she was tall, and, so he guessed, she had once been
slender instead of gaunt, before whatever sorrow had
wasted her limbs though not destroyed her beauty.
Her hands lay crossed above her breast as if a priest
were preparing her for mummification.

A young man, straight of back, with hair as black
as obsidian, knelt beside her and seized her hand and
pressed it against his cheek and tears welled out of his
eyes, and Pepy knew his father and wept for him.

"Beloved, what sorrow has stricken my wife?" The
words were wrenched from his throat like a prayer
from a man without faith.

"My lord and my lover," she whispered, and her
voice seemed to drift from the wastes and wildernesses
of the Red Desert, hollow yet musical, mingled with
wind and the mournful cry of the fennec. "It was not
in the courts of Babylon or Knossos that you found
your beloved."

"You came to me first in a dream," he said, "and
I sought your face by daylight in every city, in every
crowd. I journeyed to Knossos—sailed in a bark with

a purple moon on its prow—but found no beauty to assuage my heart. I rode on the back of an ass, like a humble merchant, to Babylon, but where were you, my dream and my intended queen, in temple or palace court? In every flame, I saw the sweet configuration of your face, in every wind I heard a voice more musical than any lyre. Will-O'-the-Wisp was only and always you."

"And you found me—where?"

"Here in this palace, bseide the pool of blue lotuses. I called you Forget-Me-Not because you stood among flowers, and the flowers seemed to spring from your steps."

"And you never asked me from where I had come."

"I never cared from where you had come. A queen or a serving girl, what did it matter to me?"

"And you wed me before the assembled might of Egypt, the kings of Babylon, and led me to your couch. Have I not been a loving wife to you?"

"No daylight has ever diminished the dream."

"And I bore you a daughter and son. Red-haired Henna, unbeautiful but skilled in the ancient ways. Red-haired Pepy with eyes as blue as the blue centaurea. Is he not unspeakably dear to you, as to me? When he lifted your heavy scepter, he, who had scarcely learned to walk, I saw you smile. When he stepped on a thorn and you cut it out of his foot and he did not cry, I saw you watch him with pride."

"You and he and Henna. Dearer than—"

"Egypt?"

He paused and anguish became his face and Pepy wanted to seize his hand and, defeating time, cry a comfort to him, "Father, Father, it is I, Pepy, and I have come to companion you."

But Pepy I proceeded inexorably, like a priest reciting an incantation, moved by a power beyond and above him, to speak the unretractable words, "I am Pharaoh. My father was the eternal Ra. I am wed to my kingdom as well as my wife."

"And if you should have to choose between your wives?"

He paused, deliberating, before he spoke. The young flawless brow wrinkled like cracked porphyry. The man warred with the pharaoh. "I would choose Egypt. But the love in my heart is not divided between you. It is love compounded with love."

"It is fitting that you should love your kingdom above your family. But are you a loving husband or the tyrant who hides his tyranny under the guise of law?"

"What do you mean?" he cried. "Am I a tyrant because I drive the demons of Set into the South? The sorcerers, the magicians, the mischiefmakers? They murdered my father. A demon of fever crept into his throat. He died in a single day."

"My lord, you have wed a demon."

He shrugged with impatience and disbelief. "You speak impieties." Then kindness returned into his kind face. "Perhaps a demon has brushed you in his flight. I will bathe you in holy water."

"And kill me, my husband, for I am a succuba."

"For you are a—" He could not speak the word. Belief—resisted, belabored, at last irresistible—possessed him more surely than any demon and twisted his tongue. "A D-Daughter of Night?"

"I came to you in the night and saw the loneliness of a man who could trust no woman in all of his court, a man so high that he seemed to stand on the highest rung of the Celestial Ladder, lonely as a god, and yearned to climb down into the world of men, but he dared not take the first irrevocable step."

He turned away from her and stood in silence, fighting, it seemed, a demon more powerful than Set. Slowly he turned to face her; knelt beside her bed and gathered her in his strong and succoring arms.

"I cannot forgo you," he said. "The others must go. But you shall remain with me, your husband, and no one shall know that my queen is also a succuba. Have you not renounced your evil, nocturnal ways? You have told me so."

She smiled, or at least to Pepy she seemed to smile, though with sorrow instead of mirth, with pity and with a look as impersonal as the wind or the rain, as elemental, the look of a woman returning to the night.

"Then I am gone."

"Forget-Me-Not!"

"You will not forget me, my husband. In the dawn, you will wake and cry yourself to sleep again and dream of me. But your dreams will not be kind."

Pepy fell to his knees beside the cradle and wept, and it seemed to him that his heart would flow with the tears through his eyes, but whether he wept for his father, foredoomed to terrible dreams and an early death, or his mother, the demon, who had forsaken the many for one and dared the inimicable light of the sun, he could not say. He only knew that he wept. He only knew, as one may know in a dream, not why nor how, that his hand crept shyly forth from his body, like the feeler of a snail, and rocked the cradle on its wooden rockers.

Someone, it seemed, had laid an arm on his shoulder, and he started and looked behind him in wonder and hope, but grappled with empty air. And yet the cradle continued to rock without his hand, and someone said, as far as the chasm into the Underworld, as near as the rocking cradle.

"Pepy II is my beloved son. His father drove me

from Egypt and from my son. Tell me the name I already know."

"I am Pepy II."

The tears seemed to freeze in his eyes, the words in his throat. I am a mummy before my time, he thought. The priests have disemboweled me, the ka has fled through my throat.

"Was he right, your father?"

"He was Pharaoh."

"Was he right?"

"He was my father and I loved him, whatever he did, and still I pray to his ka."

Insistent, inevitable, she repeated the question: "Was he right?"

"No. He was very wrong. He has wronged you and hurt you and I am ashamed for him."

He felt himself folded into sleep, a child in swaddling clothes, his tears released and dried, and he whispered before he slept, for was he not Pharaoh even if also a child?

"Will you tell the god to release his waters?"

"Egypt is a cruel land."

"She is a thirsty land."

"This drought has not yet come."

"There are other thirsts."

"I will tell the god to release his waters. He is old and bored and, whatever he says, too much alone, and when I came to his cave in the night, it was easy to praise the length of his beard and win his love and exact his promise. Again I will visit him. Again I will flatter and coax him. The Nile will flood its banks, and the wheat will grow as tall as a man, and the saffron crocus will sway like a maiden dancing to a flute. Man and maiden—together they shall fecundate the barren fields."

"Forget-Me-Not," he said.

"That was your father's name for me."

"But what shall I call you then?" He could not bring himself to speak the unspeakable word. Demons deceived, bewitched, deserted. He could not risk, so he thought, another loss.

"Whatever you must."

"Whatever I must," he said. . . .

"Mother," he said, and fell into sleep like a little boy who tumbles into a nest of clover and asphodels. . . .

Chapter X

"I'm going after him," said Harkhuf.

"No," faltered Immortelle, as if she meant "perhaps." She deserved the name of her race; she looked diminished from small to minikin; her toes looked three instead of four, and her tiny horns were rosebuds fearful of light.

"Why, by Isis' amethystine nipples, not? The thing may have eaten him and Tike too. One good bite would finish both of those boys."

"Flowers don't eat little boys, do they?"

"How do you know? This isn't your country. Didn't I have to rescue you from the Black Dwarves? You're almost as much a stranger as I am."

"Yes," she admitted, fearful, fragile, gazelle in truth, though fawn and not adult, "and I don't know the country at all. Nilus, the old grouch, may have sent them into a trap. Or maybe they lost their way or met a Black Dwarf or a hungry lion." Instead of adding another "or," she began to cry. Tearful women had always annoyed him. Red eyes, running galena, loud blubberings. . . . Ti had wept copiously for the first ten years of their marriage (not that weeping had won her any concessions).

Immortelle's tears, however, were somehow different. Misty and insubstantial she looked, like a cloud

which has strayed to earth and yearns for its proper
home, the sky. (Rosebuds, fawns, clouds—were these
the words for a whore?) Impulsively he reached a
restraining hand. Reaching, he blinked and Harkhuf,
the fearless, Harkhuf, the stonehearted, knew that he
was looking *through* a mist instead of at a mist.

He pulled her to him and choked, "There, there,
my little girl, you mustn't cry," trying desperately
to hide his own emotions, his fear for Pepy, his—what?

"Why, Harkhuf, you're crying!" It was Ti, who
else? She and Tutu, holding hands in the manner they
liked to affect, had completely materialized; Tutu had
taught Ti a scroll of tricks, it seemed. He wished her
dunked in a Delta rivulet (though without any crocodiles. Age, it appeared, had made him tolerant).

"We'll both go," said Immortelle before Ti could
add insult to disclosure. "Harkhuf and I. Tutu, do you
and Ti feel the emanation?"

Tutu, looking more manly than Harkhuf had ever
seen him, not so much soft as well-proportioned and
smooth, a golden brother to Immortelle, shook his
head. If he weren't such a sentimentalist (and of course
a jinn), I would ask him to join my explorations,
thought Harkhuf. Perhaps I could teach him better
taste in women.

"I did at first. Ti too. It was like the heat from a
brush fire in the veldt. Not any more."

"Not any more," said Ti, flushed and breathless, as
if she had come from a journey or a plot.

Harkhuf emerged gingerly from the parasol protection of the tree veronica. "Neither do I. I think we
can all go."

"*Go where?*" Pepy and Tike laughed like little boys
who have watched a magician raise a man from the
dead. Between them trotted an animal with the wings
of a bennu and the head of a lion.

"We've already been," said Pepy.

"Where's dinner?" asked Tike. "We've another mouth to feed."

"You see," said Pepy, "after my father drove my mother into Yam, she went to live in the Lotus. She grieved—can you blame her?—and miles away the Minikins felt her grief. Our friend with the wings was her only company." The sphinx, like all of its race, was stubbornly neutral in sex. The creatures reproduced after dining on flowers called Love-in-a-Mist. To judge from its snaps and growls, Pepy's sphinx had dinner in mind and possibly reproduction.

"Down, boy," said Harkhuf, narrowly recovering his hand. He prided himself on his way with a hunting dog, but this was a cat sort of thing. "I gather your mother wanted revenge," he resumed to Pepy with one eye on the sphinx. "Being a woman, that is. She brooded in her flower, she plotted, she bided her time until—"

"You came to Yam with the ka of Ti in your ring."

"And Ti and your mother got together—I'm still unclear how a ka can move so fast—and the two women decided to punish Egypt. Typical of a female. She feels herself wronged by a man and wants to punish his country."

"But Harkhuf, why were you in particular called to the flower? Did you ever wrong my mother? You never mentioned her to me at any time."

"I should hope not. I hardly knew the woman. It was before he married her that your father and I made our expeditions together. Afterwards, he stayed at home with *her* and I went alone. Calling me to the flower was Ti's idea, no doubt. For some unaccountable reason, my own dear wife has never liked me, you know."

"I didn't know, but now I do," said Pepy with the air of Osiris, the divine judge.

"She probably said to your mother, 'Why not start our revenge on Egypt with my late husband?' And your mother, having no reason to trust husbands in general, agreed, and, as it were, put me to the rack."

"I think," said Pepy, "that what my mother really wanted was to get *me* to the flower and explain her case. The plight of her friends, the succubi and other exiled demons. You were a means to me. You could return to Egypt and tell me about the bed and the cradle. Make me curious. Eager to see the flower for myself."

"Most of all," said Immortelle, "she wanted a sight of her son. More than revenge or a chance to explain anything."

"Well, she certainly took drastic measures," muttered Harkhuf. "Bribing Nilus. Dispatching a phoenix to Egypt ahead of his time. Threatening drought and famine."

"But they worked," said Pepy. "With a river god for a friend, they were bound to work. I don't think she ever meant Nilus to carry through his threat."

"I don't either," said Immortelle. "*I* wouldn't in her place."

Women and children, thought Harkhuf. Like magic, they are illogical and inexplicable. Arguments, logic, reason beat as uselessly on their ears as darts against rhinoceros hide. Pepy is still a child in spite of his manly talk. Well, no need to fire another dart.

"Perhaps you're right," he said. "But Pepy. Do you dislike your father for what he did to your mother?"

"Oh, Harkhuf, how could you think such a thing? After he sent her away, he was lonely too. That's why he took such chances against the Bedouins, don't you see. That's why he lost his life. I love both of my parents. Loving a second person needn't subtract from the first, it may even add."

"You think your father was wrong, don't you, for exiling your mother?"

"Yes, but what has wrongness to do with love? I love you, don't I?"

Before he could puzzle his pharaoh's meaning, Immortelle smiled and took Pepy's hand. "You were always good at addition."

They returned to Egypt under the climbing Dog-Star, Sothis, and with the rise of the Nile. In a village above the First Cataract, they landed their rocs and Pepy ordered a barge, one of those vessels made for carrying stone from the quarries to temple or pyramid sites, to be cleaned and gilded and equipped with oars and a canopy. The villagers of the place were quick to obey the young Pharaoh who had departed from Egypt to prevent a drought and returned with a rising river and a bumptious sphinx.

"Why not fly all the way to Chemmis?" asked Harkhuf. A voyage with Immortelle posed a curious threat. Doubts, fears, *wants* tiptoed in and out of his brain like sly Black Dwarves.

"Because," said Pepy, with the confidence of his new authority, "you had to leave your men in Yam to return by foot, and I have no army in Chemmis. Henna is there with her priests. We must gather men as we go."

"There will be no Dedwens along the riverbank."

"No, but there will be those who love magic."

The army gathered itself to greet the barge, which, afloat like a phoenix on the rising river, spoke more eloquently than cumbersome rocs of a god-decreed reprieve from drought and famine, and Pharaoh as god's own son.

"You see," Pepy cried, "they're waving to us! Tike, wave back. Your mind's with your civet cat, I can tell. But these are our *subjects*." Tike had brought a civet from Aquamarine as company for the sphinx. Secretly, he appeared to hope for a "What Have You" between the pair, though the sphinx had failed to reproduce even when gorged on Love-in-a-Mist.

Waving and shouting too, the farmers came from the huts where they ground their flour and plaited baskets in the time when there were no seeds to sow, the artisans from their hearths and tables and tools. . . . Mothers and children too, little boys who dreamed of becoming pharaoh, little girls who dreamed of marrying Pharaoh and ruling his other wives. Some came to welcome Immortelle, the Golden Minikin, and lift their arms in the immemorial gesture of adoration, for she looked like a goddess, hammered of gold and lapis lazuli, but soft, soft like flax—Hathor's daughter, without the head of a cow and come to disport with men; and some came to welcome Harkhuf, the gallant explorer, and ask him if he had brought any elephants out of Yam or ridden an ostrich or climbed the sloping tower of a—what was the name of the beast?—a giraffe's neck, and he grinned and patted the indeterminate Sphinx, which lashed its tail and growled, and the people shuddered and laughed and clapped their hands at the sight of magic returning from the South.

But mostly they stared at Pepy, and Harkhuf was proud to hear them say,

"He's taller than when he left."

"He doesn't even wear a wig but he seems to be crowned. See how he glows!"

"He looks like his father, except he's not so stern, and he has his mother's hair. . . ."

Pepy waved merrily and seized Tike's hand—no one,

it seemed, had noticed the fisherboy—and called to the crowd,

"This is my new court musician!"

"Sing us a song, Court Musician," they shouted, those on the shore. "Sing us a river tune to go with the slap, slap, slap of the oars, and to honor Pharaoh's return and the risen Nile," and Tike sang an ancient river song, older than either of the Twin Kingdoms, rhymed in the way of the oldest songs; and Harkhuf tried to accompany him on a flute, though lacking patience he was a poor musician. Still, the sound of the oars and the river and Tike's words were music for any song:

THE RIVER GOD

God of the river,
Sandaled with blue rain,
Purple the grapes until they tempt the bees
To rich and clustered ease
And, swelling barley, undulate the plain!

God of the river,
Sandal-less and shorn,
Crouch in a brackish pool to shirk the sun
While rust and locusts run
Implacable among your broken corn.

God of the river, loved in your largesse:
Shall losing you make you less?

Tutu and Ti insisted on remaining invisible, presumably perched on the prow (and certainly hand in hand). Perhaps they did not wish to materialize before a crowd; perhaps they possessed a remnant of shame and did not wish to display their disgusting passion aboard a pharaoh's barge and in the sight of his people.

Nevertheless, Harkhuf heard them whisper together like children or lovers.

"Is it well with you, my love?" asked Tutu. "Egypt has been the country of your grief."

Ti answered him dreamily—Harkhuf strained to overhear her words and, in spite of himself, he saw her in his imagination, soft, with russet hair and slender hands and Cretan skirt like an upturned lotus blossom.

"My country is love, and love is you."

Harkhuf frowned. No wonder she had taken to acting like a temple virgin. Tutu was spoiling her with the fatuous manners of his profession.

But Pepy, listening, smiled, and Harkhuf was glad for him. Illusions were good for the young.

Meanwhile, the crowds multiplied like an army which draws recruits from every hamlet, and followed the barge and the river, carrying tools—hoe, scythe, ax—which could also be used as weapons; the crowds in fact had become the largest army since Narmer had joined the Twin Kingdoms, and word of its march would anticipate Pepy in the tiny boats which spurted ahead of the barge like waterbugs, and come to the ears of Henna and Ayub, and make them count their misdeeds and look to their necks!

Soon the chirping of individuals yielded to a great unanimous cry. At first Harkhuf took it to be a lamentation like the one which he remembered from the time when he had watched the demons departing from Egypt. It was just as loud; it seemed to cover the countryside like a plague of locusts. No. Crickets instead of locusts, exaltation instead of lamentation, though whether it issued from the welcoming people or the returning demons, who could say? Still, it was a joyful sound.

And so they came to Chemmis, and Henna, attended by the ugliest ladies of the court, greeted them as they left the barge. The ladies in beehive wigs suggested an apiary. When Henna bowed to her brother, her wig fell into the water and showed the thin carroty red of her natural hair, and she seemed to Harkhuf a poor, graceless thing whom no man could love, and thus he could understand her ambition, which unloved women sometimes take in place of lovers, and wondered if Pepy would recognize her loss and forgive her treachery.

"Never mind, Sister," said Pepy, lifting her beside him and replacing the wig. "I *won't* marry you, Osiris be my witness, but I won't imprison you either, and you don't have to watch for vipers." In her own way, thought Harkhuf, she has helped him to serve their mother. The kind of magic she tried to restore was dark and cruel, the dark side of Set. Still, it was part of the One.

She pressed a tremulous cheek to her brother's face and galena ran from her eyes in green rivulets.

"Henna," said Immortelle, drawing the princess away from Pepy before the galena could turn him green. "I must teach you the proper use of a cosmetic palette. You do yourself an injustice. Do you want to look like an ass instead of a princess?"

At first Henna glared at her, as if she would like to shout, "Off to the crocodiles!" Then she blushed and stammered, "Y-you mean you see possibilities?"

"Probabilities," said Immortelle. "First you must choose a wig which complements the contours of your face. A beehive is only good for an oval face."

"And a face like mine? An asinine face?"

"Something soft and fluffy and loose. Then you will be a gazelle instead of an ass."

"I should like that," said Henna, and, for the first

time in Harkhuf's memory, she lapsed into a bemused and contented silence.

"But Ayub," said Pepy, continuing his judgment, "it was not Set and his demons you served, it was yourself. You would have killed me to get my throne. For you there must be a punishment suitable to the crime. I, Pharaoh whom you tried to poison, hereby decree—"

For the first time, Harkhuf noticed the priest of Anubis, the jackal-god, standing unobserved in the crowd behind Ayub, faintly smiling; anticipatory.

Pepy, following Harkhuf's gaze, started as if a terror had climbed into his throat. He touched Harkhuf's arm and asked a puzzling question,

"Has the god come for me?"

"The god?" repeated Harkhuf. "The priest of Anubis, you mean?"

Ayub, scornful, handsome, utterly unrepentant, hair as black as onyx, copper blade at his side, smiled at the boy who seemed to waver in sentencing him to die.

The priest who was dressed like a jackal touched Ayub's shoulder and Ayub turned and flinched and looked like wet papyrus, and the two priests, inseparable as lovers, lost themselves in the crowd. . . .

And so it is ended, thought Harkhuf, and, thanks to the women, there is neither drought nor famine in Egypt, demons and magic have returned from the South, and Pepy is king in truth without any further need of me. Only I am free. Only I have not been arranged into a kingdom's destiny, or even that of another wife. Someone has done her best to arrange my heart and, given a few more days . . . but days are meant for the road, the river, the sea! Knossos or

Punt or Babylon! Apes and ivory, incense and gold and myrrh. . . .

"And my loyal subject Harkhuf," Pepy was saying. "I reward him with a new estate on Elephantine."

A popular decision. Approval was spontaneous and instantaneous. Harkhuf beamed at the prospect of new revenues to finance his expedition. Instead of a ship, a fleet. . . .

"However—"

However? Harkhuf would have preferred a simple "and."

"However, for a crime I choose not to name, I hereby sentence him to a year's exile."

Could Harkhuf believe his ears or had too many sandstorms left him deaf?

"Pepy," he cried. "What have I done?"

"You were careless once in a boat," said Pepy, then to his people, "I sentence him to a year's exile on the island of Sappharine."

"But how shall I get there? The rocks, the monsters . . ."

"Immortelle will guide you. She may even lend you a roc."

Arrangements! Between them, the women had reached him through his king.

"By Hathor's bosom, she won't—"

"Indeed, I won't," she snapped. "Pharaoh has no power to command *me*, a Minikin. *I* am not his subject. What is more, I expect to be promoted from Whore to Courtesan when I return to my homeland."

"Perhaps," suggested Harkhuf, reconsidering. If he *must* go into exile—and Pepy's look said yes—if he *must* go to Sappharine on the back of a roc, he needed a guide. Certainly he needed a guide. Immortelle was bewitching to the eye, melodious to the ear. He liked her horns, he liked her diminution, he liked her four-toed feet. She knew how to handle a roc on the wing. She could sing and dance and cook and swim and explore (and wench). In fact, she was good at everything except fulfilling Hathor's intention for women; that is to say, cultivating obedience to men.

"Yes, Harkhuf?" There was still asperity in the question; less, perhaps, than in her "indeed."

"Part of the way?"

"If you choose to follow me to Sappharine, that is your choice," she said, without, however, an invitation.

"Accompany you?"

"I shall give it some thought."

"Must you exude that damnable musk? It has quite clogged my senses."

"I only exude when I wish to allure."

"*Something* has gone to my head. I can't think clearly at all."

"I imagine it will be your greatest adventure," said a voice from his ring. Ha! Ti had returned to her nest to observe and relish his public humiliation.

"Yes," he barked. "The furthest, to the strangest land. Monsters and clashing rocks. I shall probably die or lose an arm or leg." He waited for the predictable bitterness, the taunt, the recrimination.

"That's not what I mean," said Ti. "That's not at all what I mean."

"Just what *do* you mean?"

The ring felt suddenly lighter on his finger. Women! Why could they never say what they meant like men? He had never been good at riddles.

"Immortelle," he asked. "Did you hear what Ti just said to me?"

"Yes."

"Do you know what she meant?"

"Yes."

"What?"

"I think you already know."

"Do I?" The memory of musk, if not its presence, had certainly gone to his head, or else the gold of her hair, or else the nipples which seemed to wink at him through the blue transparent gown. "Yes, I suppose I do. But how did *you* know?"

"It came with my education."

"I won't have you call yourself a whore!"

"Can you suggest a better occupation?"

A great adventurer, he opened his arms to his greatest adventure.

EPILOGUE

Pepy was sad. It was the sadness which came from the absence of Harkhuf and Immortelle. It was the sadness of leaving wonder for duty, renouncing even Harpocrates in order to rule by night as well as day. He had freed his Nubian slave, Jacinth, and restored him to Nubia as a prince. Tutu and Ti were welcome friends when they chose to materialize, but they hurried into invisibility at the first chance, enrapt in each other, merely dutiful to their king. Tike was friend as well as court musician, but he kept a special place in his heart, a kind of halcyon nest, where he found his songs, and Pepy tried in vain to follow him. Even the sphinx and the civet cat had chosen to live in a temple instead of the palace and share the burnt offerings with the priests.

He thought of paying a visit to a local whore, but who could sing and dance like Immortelle? He thought reluctantly of marriage, but he knew that the merest mention of such a project would lead his people, who liked what they chose to call consanguinity, to suggest his sister as his first bride.

Thus it was, lonely, wanting to talk but finding no one to listen, that he walked into the courtyard where he had overheard the plot to take his life. He looked at the path of crushed coquina shells. He looked at the palm trees, laden with fruit like multifarious breasts of Hathor. He looked at the lotuses in the pool, blue and pink and white and, one of them, a newcomer, brightest among the bright, tallest among the tall,

Green.

ACKNOWLEDGMENTS

I wish to acknowledge a particular debt to Margaret A. Murray's *The Splendor That Was Egypt*, a lucid and altogether excellent book for beginning Egyptologists like me: Jon Manchip White's *Everyday Life in Ancient Egypt*, a book ostensibly for children but so graceful in style and rich in lore that its publisher would be wise to promote it for all ages; and *Egyptian Mythology*, a book which suffers because it was written by several authors but serves, nonetheless, both in its pictures and in its text, to introduce the principal Egyptian gods.

The Prayer to Wenis, the Bull of the Sky, is quoted from Margaret A. Murray's book. The letter from the young pharaoh, Pepy II, to his caravan leader, Harkhuf, in which the boy asks to be brought a dancing dwarf from Yam, is an actual historical document dating from the Old Kingdom.* The poems and the light verses are my own. "Ibis" is reprinted with the permission of *The New York Times* and "Ask the Wind," with the permission of *Wings*.

---

*A note of possible interest—Pepy II reigned over Egypt for more than ninety years, the longest reign in recorded history.

DAW PRESENTS THOMAS BURNETT SWANN

An utterly unique writer of fantasies and imaginative legen-
dry. . . .

☐ **GREEN PHOENIX.** A tour de force of the final stronghold
of the prehumans of the Wanderwood and of their strange
defense against the last legion of fallen Troy.
(#UY1222—$1.25)

☐ **HOW ARE THE MIGHTY FALLEN.** A fantasy-historical
tapestry of a queen of ancient Judea who was more than
human, her son who became legend, and the Cyclopean
nemesis whose name became synonymous with colossus.
(#Q1100—95¢)

☐ **THE NOT-WORLD.** The story of a strange balloon flight
that brought three English venturers into an older and
more enchanted land to mingle their fates with the last
of the weird folk. (#UY1158—$1.25)

Presenting the international science fiction spectrum:

☐ **STAR (PSI CASSIOPEIA)** by C. I. Defontenay. The first epic novel of interstellar civilization, rediscovered for today's readers. (#UY1200—$1.25)

☐ **THE ENCHANTED PLANET** by Pierre Barbet. Intergalactic sword & sorcery by a leading French sf novelist. (#UY1181—$1.25)

☐ **GAMES PSYBORGS PLAY** by Pierre Barbet. They made a whole world their arena and a whole race their pawns. (#UQ1087—95¢)

☐ **STARMASTERS' GAMBIT** by Gerard Klein. Games players of the cosmos—an interstellar adventure equal to the best. (#UQ1068—95¢)

☐ **THE ORCHID CAGE** by Herbert W. Franke. The problem of robots and intelligence as confronted by Germany's master of hard-core science fiction. (#UQ1082—95¢)

☐ **2018 A.D. OR THE KING KONG BLUES** by Sam J. Lundwall. A shocker in the tradition of A Clockwork Orange. (#UY1161—$1.25)

☐ **HARD TO BE A GOD** by A. & B. Strugatski. A brilliant novel of advanced men on a backward planet—by Russia's most outstanding sf writers. (#UY1141—$1.25)

☐ **THE MIND NET** by Herbert W. Franke. Their starship was kidnapped by an alien brain from a long-dead world. (#UQ1136—95¢)

DAW BOOKS are represented by the publishers of Signet and Mentor Books, **THE NEW AMERICAN LIBRARY, INC.**

THE NEW AMERICAN LIBRARY, INC.,
P.O. Box 999, Bergenfield, New Jersey 07621

Please send me the DAW BOOKS I have checked above. I am enclosing
$_____(check or money order—no currency or C.O.D.'s).
Please include the list price plus 25¢ a copy to cover mailing costs.

Name_____

Address_____

City_____State_____Zip Code_____
Please allow at least 3 weeks for delivery